TAMING WILD HEARTS

SCARLET ROBBINS

Tigress Books

Copyright @ 2022 by Scarlet Robbins (HJD)

ISBN/SKU - 978-1-0879-0337-8
EISBN - 978-1-0879-2904-0

All rights reserved. No part of this book may be reproduced in any manner whatsoever without written permission except in the case of brief quotations embodied in critical articles and reviews. This book is a work of fiction. Names, characters, places, and incidents are fictitious. Any resemblances to actual persons, living or dead, events, or locales is entirely coincidental.

First Printing, 2022

TAMING WILD HEARTS

Dedicated to *my* favorite, sexy, bad-boy musicians:

Paul Stanley (KISS) - Forever My Handsome Starchild, Hold Me, Touch Me, (Think of Me When We're Apart)

Eric Carr (KISS) - Always my Little Caesar - RIP Gentle Soul

Michael Nesmith (The Monkees, The First National Band) - Forever My Papa Nez, running from the Grand Ennui beneath the lonely light of the Silver Moon

Peter Steele (Type-O-Negative) - My Sexy Black Number One - RIP Dear Heart

Glenn Danzig (Misfits, Samhain, Danzig) - Come Burn with Me in The Violet Fire

Alfred "Weird Al" Yankovic - Forever and Always My Beautiful Bologna, Living With a Hernia at the Hardware Store on a Bad Hair Day

Thank you for the memories. Thank you for always being near and by my side. I love you all!

PROLOGUE

My body writhed against the silk bed sheets as a fourth orgasm tore through it. The remnants of our lovemaking clear by the drying puddles it created. Every nerve ending from the depths of my pussy, to the top of my head, was on fire. My fingers wrapped tighter around the intricate scrolling adorning the iron headboard, causing the cool steel of the handcuffs to cut deeper into my tender flesh. The candles surrounding the room were on the verge of extinguishment and the dissipating smell of vanilla musk, mixed with sex, filled the air. Fresh tears streamed down my face joining the trail of dried ones.

"Please... I... can't."

My mind cried to end the torture and the pleas from my lips became mere whimpers. His strong, calloused hand grabbed my sopping mound, squeezing it. The low growl that escaped his lips filled me with both fear and excitement.

"No bitch... now say it... who does this pussy belong to?"

Just when I thought I couldn't take anymore, he pushed my body further to the limit. I was an instrument in his own personal concerto. It was what I craved. It was what he craved. We couldn't live without it. His hand slid higher, across my stomach, to both of my breasts, skimming them before tightening around the delicate structure of my throat. A bolt of lightning flashed in his dark eyes.

"I *said* who do you belong to?!"

Our mutual addiction to pain threatened to consume us. Not only physically, but also emotionally. He now owned my body, my heart and quite possibly my soul. I would do anything for him.

As my eyes fluttered shut, the words flowed like fine wine. "Grayson..."

I would do anything for my Master.

CHAPTER ONE

"Good morning Chicago! Time to rise and shine, sleepyheads," my alarm clock blared, jolting me from my dreamworld. I rolled over, slammed my hand against the off button, and looked at its red digits. Seven-thirty. Shit. I'm gonna be late. I really needed to get more sleep. Jumping out of my bed, I headed to the bathroom. After peeing, brushing my teeth, and taking a quick shower, I rummaged through my closet for an outfit. I settled on my light lavender blouse, black skirt, and black knee-high boots. I returned to the bathroom, put my long brown hair up into a neat ponytail, and quickly applied my makeup. After a once-over in the mirror and a quick spritz of my vanilla scented perfume, I headed downstairs to the kitchen. Throwing open a cabinet door, I grabbed a strawberry Pop-Tart before flinging my purse over my shoulder and heading out the door into the waiting world. The sun's morning rays greeted me as I headed to my Firebird. I jumped in and cranked the engine. This car was amazing, and it was my baby. I popped in my "70's Rock Super Hits" cassette tape and as the awesome sounds of Bad Company blared from the speakers, I headed off to another fun filled day of... work.

I'm an Administrative Assistant for a law firm just outside of Chicago. I've been here for almost five years. My boss is an ass. He's built like a linebacker and struts around in Armani suits, Italian loafers, and expensive cologne, which smells like cat piss. He thinks his shit doesn't stink because he has money and clout. There are more important things in life. He thinks I'm his lackey and nit-picks everything I do. I hate it, but I put up with his bullshit because I need my job and the money is good. One day my ship will come in, but I will probably be at the airport.

I arrived at work with five minutes to spare and sat down at my desk. After logging onto my computer, I began munching on my Pop-Tart. After the second bite, my nosy co-worker Dottie strolled by. She's been here for twenty-three years and is in everyone's business. Telephone, tell-a-friend, tell Dottie. She is always accusing me of not doing my job. She swears that she's the perfect employee. Pfft.

"Good Morning Violet."

Speak of the devil.

"Mornin' Dottie," I grumbled.

"Aww, what's the matter? Did you get up on the wrong side of the bed again?" A sarcastic chuckled escaped her. "Or should I say, woke up in an empty bed."

I furrowed my brows and scowled at her. "Shut up Dottie."

She sauntered over to my desk and planted her ass on it. "Ya know, Violet, like I keep sayin', you really need to get laid. Cause work sure ain't puttin' any smiles on that mug of yours." She tapped her nails on my desk. "And you wonder why the boss is always on your case!"

My temper flared, and I could feel the anger rising in my chest. "And you know what, Dottie? Last time I checked, my face AND my sex life were none of your damn business!" I spat it right back at her.

Dottie threw her hands up in defeat and hopped off my desk. "Fine, I'm leavin'. Have a nice day," she snickered.

I sighed heavily and fixed my eyes back on my computer screen. "Bitch."

"I heard that!"

"Good!"

As I continued to finish the report for my boss's afternoon meeting, Dottie's words danced around in my head. I don't know why I let her get to me. She didn't know it, but she was right. I hadn't been with anyone since... yeah, that was another story for another time. I had learned how to stand on my own two feet now and I wouldn't take shit from anyone.

Around twelve-thirty, my stomach reminded me it was lunchtime. I grabbed the report off the printer, headed to my boss's office, and knocked on the door.

"Come in Violet," he called.

"Sir, here is your report."

"Good. You can lay it here on my desk. I trust there aren't any mistakes? You know I'm meeting with the Bernard firm and I don't want to be embarrassed!"

I laid the warm stack of colorful papers on his desk. "No sir, there shouldn't be any problems. I know how important this deal is for you."

"Good!"

"If there is nothing else, sir, I'm going to lunch now." I turned around to leave when he stopped me. Damn, almost made it.

"Wait Violet, I do have something else I need you to do for me."

I placed my hand on my stomach as more hunger pains ravaged it. Great.

"Yes, sir, what is that?"

"I need you to acquire two tickets to the upcoming benefit concert at the UIC Pavilion on Saturday night. My wife is a huge Rancid Orchid fan and I want to surprise her."

I looked at him like he had three heads. "Rancid Orchid, sir?" I wanted to make sure I had heard him correctly. I was prepared to hear him say Mozart or Beethoven. Hell, even Willie Nelson, but Rancid Orchid? Biff and Buffy Cartwell sure didn't look like headbangers.

Biff wrinkled his nose and looked taken aback by my questioning. "Yes Violet, Rancid Orchid, the rock band. They are giving a benefit concert for the poor and unfortunate."

Was this dumbass serious? He even fingered air quotation marks as he said the last part.

"Well sir, with all due respect, I will try to get them. But I mean, it's already Thursday and there may not be any-"

He cut me off. "Just do what you have to do," he said, shooing his hand at me. "And close the door on your way out!"

I scurried away like a timid mouse and pulled the door shut behind me. Walking back to my desk, I waved my hand at the door in a mocking gesture. *Do what you have to do.* Jackass. How the hell was I going to pull this off? My stomach protested again. I guess I'll figure something out. Right now, there was something more important to attend to... lunch.

CHAPTER TWO

My boots clicked against the sidewalk as I rounded the corner to Roy's neighborhood deli. I ran in long enough to grab a turkey sandwich, a bag of chips, and an orange Crush. My favorite. The sky was growing dark and thunder rumbled in the distance so I hurried back to the office before the downpour started. I slid back into my chair with ten minutes to spare. I relished in the first bite of my sandwich and a cold gulp of my soda. It hit the spot. Now, it was time to get my ass in gear and find these non-existent tickets.

I started first by calling the pavilion box office. Which, to no surprise, didn't have any available. Next, I looked through the newspaper to see if anyone was selling theirs. And of course they weren't. My only other option was to see if I could find a scalper. I seriously considered this option for about ten seconds. Biff may have told me to do what I had to do, but neither he nor Buffy were worth me being put in potential danger or getting thrown in jail.

Why did he want these tickets so bad, anyway? He may have said that he wanted them for his wife, but knowing Biff, there was more to it. And were Rancid Orchid still that popular? I mean, I knew who they were, and I had some of their early records. I heard about the wild bad boy antics and sex scandals surrounding their leader Grayson Maddox. Who didn't know that guy? But now, we were living in the new millennium. I could have passed the guy on the street and wouldn't have taken a second look. As I took another bite of my sandwich, my desk phone started ringing.

"Thank you for calling The Cartwell Agency. This is Violet how can I help you?"

"Violet, it's Biff."

I rolled my eyes. "Yes sir, what did you need?"

"Were you able to get the tickets I asked for?"

I paused for a moment. He wasn't going to like my answer. "Well, sir... I tried... but–"

"So what you're telling me Violet, is that once again, you did not perform the job I asked of you?" Biff huffed in my ear.

I was silent.

"I'm waiting for an answer Violet!"

If I had my way, he would've kept on waiting. "No sir. I guess I didn't."

Biff released a disappointing sigh. "Tell Dottie to get the tickets for me and let her know I'll call her later."

And with that, he slammed the phone in my ear. Oh, this was going to be fun.

I finished my lunch then walked down the hall to Dottie's desk. She saw me approaching and a shit-eating grin formed on her lips.

"What do you want?"

Don't kill her... my mind repeated on an endless loop.

"Look, bossman wanted me to get tickets to the Rancid Orchid concert on Saturday night at UIC. But they're impossible to get. So, he wants you to get them. Oh, and he said he would call you later."

Dottie laughed. "So what you're telling me, is that once again, you didn't do your job? And now, I have to clean up your mess."

My temper reared its ugly head as I slammed my hands down on her desk and looked into her crow's feet laden eyes. "Uh no, you aren't doing my job. I do my damn job, and rather well thank you! I just don't know how you're going to find what I couldn't!"

She looked up at me and laughed again. "Violet can't you just accept the fact that you are a screw-up? Life will be much easier once you do!"

I gave her one last death glare then turned around and started back to my desk. But then I stopped and turned back around with a smart-ass grin plastered on my face.

"Ya know Dottie, you might get those tickets after all."

She looked at me puzzled. "How?"

"Just pull them out of your ass!"

She was pissed now. "And I think, you need to go sit your ass down!"

I roared out in laughter and gave a little wave as I headed back to my desk. "Bye bitch!"

The rest of the day went by pretty quickly and before long it was five o'clock. I just wanted to go home, drown my cares in a glass of Merlot and dissolve into a hot bubble bath. I logged off my computer and grabbed my purse. A few minutes later, I was stepping out of the building, into the cool October air. The smell of fresh rain greeted my nose. Fall has always been my favorite season. I dashed across the parking lot to my car before another downpour hit. I wished I had brought my umbrella, but I would soon be home and it wouldn't matter.

Rush hour traffic was a nightmare. Almost an hour later, I pulled into my driveway. Home sweet home. I went inside and headed for the kitchen, silently hoping that something different had magically appeared in the refrigerator since last night. I opened the door. Nope, same shit from yesterday. Damn. I took out the leftover macaroni and put it in the microwave then went to the cupboard for a wine glass. Just as I opened it, my phone started ringing.

Grrr. "Hello."

"Hey screw-up!" Dottie smirked in my ear.

"What do you want?" I asked, pulling out a glass.

"I got the boss's tickets."

I paused and rolled my eyes. "Good for you. I'm sure he'll be happy."

The enthusiasm flowed from Dottie. "Oh, he was. In fact, he was so happy he gave me next week off with pay!"

Double grrr. I just had to know. "So how did you get them?"

"Well, I called the box office and when I told them who wanted the tickets, they pulled some strings with the Rancid Orchid team."

I felt stupid. I guess I could've done that. Oh well, it was over and done. But I had a feeling there was more to it.

"Look Dottie, what do you really want?"

"Well, since you asked so nicely... I got the tickets but there was one hitch."

I rolled my eyes again and shook my head. "And that would be?"

"I told the box office that you'd pick them up."

Oh, I was hot now. "You did what?! Why can't you get 'em? Or even better, Biff? They're his tickets!"

Dottie got loud. "Because screw-up, I did your work for you and Mr. Cartwell shouldn't have to get them when you're his assistant. That's what you get paid for remember?"

A sigh of resignation escaped my chest. "Yeah... yeah... alright. When do I have to pick them up?"

"Before eight tonight."

"WHAT?!" I looked at the clock on the kitchen wall. It was already a quarter to seven. Shit.

"Are you serious? I'll never make it in time."

Dottie snickered. "Yes, you will. It's not like you're entertaining anyone this evening!"

A low growl crossed my lips. "Alright, the sooner you shut the hell up, the sooner I can leave."

"Good! Don't screw this up!"

And with that the line went dead.

I sat my glass on the counter and left the macaroni in the microwave. I should be back sometime tonight. So much for my wine and hot bath. I grabbed my purse and drug myself back out to the car. I looked at the clock on the dashboard. It was almost seven. UIC Pavilion here I come.

CHAPTER THREE

I weaved in and out of traffic, running damn near every red-light along the way. The speed limit might have said fifty, but I saw seventy-five. There was no way I was going to make it before eight. Biff and Buffy were going to have to sit their asses outside on the grass. I glanced at the clock on the dashboard again. It was seven fifty-four. A silent prayer crossed my lips, hoping someone above would have mercy on me. Someone must have heard because my destination soon appeared on the horizon.

I turned off the main road, damn near bringing the car up onto two wheels, and zoomed into the UIC parking lot. Luckily, there were only a few cars, so I grabbed a spot near the front of the building. I parked, jumped out, and started power-walking to the box office. But the closer I got to the window, the more my worst fears became a reality. The finality of the black and red "closed" sign seared my retinas.

"NO!!" I yelled, banging on the window. "Hello?! Is anyone in there? I'm here to pick up tickets. Please, someone answer!"

And at that moment, something answered—a loud clap of thunder followed by a brilliant flash of purple. The sky opened up, and I was now stuck in the middle of a downpour. I raced to the front of the building, pulled on the door, and found it locked. Damn! I started pounding on it with all my might.

"Hello? Anyone there?" I called, desperation filling my voice.

No answer.

I moved back around the building and knocked on the window one last time. Still nothing. A heavy sigh escaped my body, and I did something I hadn't done in a long time—I cried. Dottie was right. I was a screw-up. I couldn't even do one simple task. And now I was going to be fired. What was I gonna do? The heavy drops from both my eyes and the heavens continued to fall. My drenched blouse and skirt clung to my tall frame like a second skin. My velvet boots were most likely ruined. And my ponytail holder had slid out, causing my soaked hair to curtain my face and shoulders. I looked like a drowned rat. Turning on my heels, I headed back to the car, all the while envisioning my new life, working for the golden arches with a real clown for a boss. I had taken about five steps when I thought I heard a voice.

"Uh, miss?"

I continued to walk.

"HEY GIRL!"

Now that time, I heard a voice. And this time it was yelling.

I turned around and saw the front door cracked open. The dim light in the doorway highlighted a shadowy figure.

A feeling of relief washed over me. Finally.

I sloshed over to the door and pushed the soaked strands of hair out of my eyes. The figure was a man. My eyes grazed over him. He was a tall drink of water. I guessed he was in his late forties or early fifties. A form-fitting black t-shirt, with an intricate scrolling of cyan mixed in, covered his solid torso and tummy pouch, while black jeans and red boots completed his look. I liked his style. His long chestnut hair, with gray strands peeking here and there, brushed the tips of his shoulders, while his gracefully worn face displayed a manly salt and pepper goatee, that beckoned for me to stroke it. My breath hitched in my chest. He wasn't only handsome... he was beautiful. The angels knew what they were doing when they created him. I moved in closer and looked into his eyes. A warm amber with gold flecks shined back at me. They were so soulful, so hypnotizing. And yet I couldn't help but notice the sadness that was hidden deep. If someone wasn't careful, they could easily fall under their spell. I was still staring when the stranger's voice suddenly brought me back to reality.

"Would you like to come in out of the rain?"

His voice was deep like a canyon and smooth like fine silk.

"Uh yeah, sorry." I said, stepping through the door, lightly brushing against him.

The heavy door slammed shut, and he turned to face me. "I didn't know if you heard me calling you. I'm glad you did." A gentle smile graced his pouty lips.

"How did you know I was out there?"

"I heard someone pounding on the door and I investigated."

"Oh."

He wrinkled his face. "Why are you wandering around in an empty parking lot, anyway?"

"It's a long story." I sighed.

The stranger ran his hand through his soft looking locks. "I got time."

A shiver ran down my spine. "Well," I began, "my boss wanted me to get him tickets for the concert Rancid Orchid is having on Saturday. So, I tried everywhere to get them."

The stranger looked at me inquisitively. "So did you?"

"No, they're sold out. And when I told my boss, he was upset with me and asked my co-worker to get them instead."

"Yeah, I heard they went like hot cakes," he snickered. "Did your co-worker get them?"

"Yeah. Apparently, she pulled some strings with Rancid Orchid's team and... viola." I threw my hands up in mock excitement.

The stranger nodded his head and lightly chuckled. "Hmm, must be nice to have friends in high places."

"I guess. Anyway, she told me since she got the tickets, I had to pick them up before eight tonight. But when I got here, the box office had already closed."

Outside, the storm continued to rage. But inside, there was an awkward silence now between us. I watched as his eyes left mine and slowly skimmed over the length of my body. Self-consciousness washed over me as I suddenly realized that he could see the outline of my breasts, my stiff nipples, through my wet shirt. The air in the room thickened. I quickly crossed my arms in front of myself and he darted his eyes back to mine.

"So... whatcha ya gonna do?" he asked nonchalantly.

I shook my head. "I don't know. I have no tickets and tomorrow I will have no job." My body was on the verge of tears again, but I wouldn't let him see them fall.

"That's a shame," the stranger said, a hint of care tinged in his voice. I knew he could see the disappointment filling my eyes.

"Look," he began, "it'll be ok."

I searched his eyes, hoping there was some kind of truth to his words.

"No, it won't."

He moved toward me, shortening the distance between us until we were mere inches apart. "Yes, it will." His reassuring words lightly caressed my face. "Go have a seat over by the soda machine and I'll be right back."

He turned, and I watched him walk away down a long corridor. I didn't know if he was really coming back. He seemed sincere. I sat down in the small chair next to the Pepsi machine. My body was freezing from being in my wet clothes for so long. I just wanted to climb into a nice hot bath and forget about life. The air conditioning unit kicked on and goosebumps spread across my skin as I started shivering. I thought about getting up and leaving. I wasn't sure how much time had passed and just when I thought he had forgotten about me, he suddenly returned.

"Here," he said, offering me a towel. "I thought you could use this."

I took the plush royal blue linen and scrunched it first through my dripping hair. "Thank you. That was nice of you." I then placed it around my shoulders, hoping to fight off the coldness.

Sincerity flavored his words. "You're welcome. And here," he handed me a white envelope, "I thought you could use these too."

I opened it and inside were two tickets to the Rancid Orchid concert with a VIP party afterward. Both shock and joy overcame me.

"Oh my God! How did you get these? Thank you!" I gushed, jumping up from my chair, the towel falling to the floor. Without thinking, I moved to give him a hug, and he instantly backed away.

"Whoa there, sweetheart, watch the clothes."

A splash of red suddenly painted my cheeks. "Sorry about that."

"It's cool." he said, smoothing out his shirt then picking up the towel.

"I don't know how you did this, but I will repay you somehow. You saved my ass!"

He smiled like the Cheshire cat. "Well..." he smirked, then cleared his throat. "I'm glad I could help you out. Hopefully, your boss won't fire you now."

"I hope not!"

"Look, this has been fun and all, but I gotta get back to rehears — uh work." The stranger walked over to the door and cracked it open, peering outside. "Looks like the rain stopped."

"Oh, yeah, well, I guess I should get going then." I mumbled, walking toward the door.

I stuck out my hand to shake his. "Thanks again Mr. uh..."

"Bertram. You can call me Mr. Bertram. And you're very welcome Miss…"

"Deveraux, Violet Deveraux."

He delicately grasped my hand and brought it to his lips. "Until we meet again, Miss Violet."

"Until then Mr. Bertram." I responded, moving past him, stepping through the doorway.

When I got halfway across the parking lot, I turned back to see if he was still there. He wasn't. I made it back to my car and climbed in, placing the tickets in my purse. Looking down at my hand, I lightly skimmed my fingers over the spot he had kissed. I enjoyed the feel of his lips on my flesh. It was a shame I would never see him again. I may have been in a pissed off mood all day, but things had turned around. It was time to finish my macaroni and my wine. And it was time to climb into my hot bath and think about Mr. Bertram.

CHAPTER FOUR

I strolled into the office the next morning with pep in my step. It's amazing what a bottle of wine, a relaxing bath, and thoughts of a sexy man can do. And it was Friday. Thank God. I had the boss's tickets tucked away in my purse and was ready to take on the world. As I sat down at my desk, I spied Dottie headed in my direction. I hoped her A-game was on point today because I was ready.

"Well, if it isn't ol' sour puss!"

"Hag," I spat, logging onto my computer.

A smug grin spread across her wrinkled face. "Did you get the tickets?"

I knew she was waiting for me to admit defeat, but my confidence radiated. "I sure did!"

Dottie moved to the middle of the floor and started clapping. "You hear that, everyone? Screw-up did something right for once!" Some of my fellow co-workers joined in her mock celebration.

I tried to ignore them, but my blood pressure was boiling. "You know what Dottie? Fuck you!"

Her face twisted into a fake frown. "Oh my, did I hit a nerve? Poor baby."

Dottie's mouth continued to move, but I didn't hear a word she was saying. My eyes lapsed into tunnel vision as I stared a hole through her. A small quake spread across my body, causing my hands and legs to convulse. There is only so much a person can take. And when they finally reach that breaking point, heaven can only help whatever or whoever is in their way. Something deep down inside of me snapped and before I realized it, I was stalking around my desk like a panther toward her. The laughter spilling from her mouth suddenly turned to silence as I inched closer.

"What the hell do you think you're doing?" she nervously questioned, taking a step back.

My eyes continued to bore into her as I took another step forward. If looks could have killed, she would've been in a body bag today.

"Have you lost your damn mind, Violet?"

At that moment, I probably had. Dottie continued to slink backwards, and a dark laugh escaped me as I watched her trip over the flowerpot by the front door. Regaining her balance, her body finally connected with the wall behind her. She darted her eyes up at me. The fear and uncertainty clouding them was priceless. This was my chance, and I was taking it. I leaned down and placed my face inches from hers. I could've sworn she had a familiar odor of cat piss on her.

"What I'm doing, Dottie, is telling you that if you don't leave me the fuck alone, I promise I will hurt you. I have put up with your shit for five years now and I'm tired of it. So you better start respecting me, or you just might be retiring earlier than you expected."

She looked like a deer caught in a pair of high beams. Beep beep Dorothy.

"Do you understand me?"

Her head bobbed up and down like one of those dolls in the back window of a car.

"Good. I'm glad we have an understanding."

I heard the ding of the elevator out in the hallway and saw Biff stepping out, heading toward the front door. I moved away from Dottie and she rushed past me, headed toward her desk.

"Oh, and Dottie," I called to her before she was out of earshot.

She stopped and turned to look at me.

"Remember, karma is a bitch... and her name is Violet." I puckered my lips and blew her a kiss. Muah.

She turned back around and scurried down the hallway.

I took a deep breath and went back to my desk. As I silently applauded my courage and tried to calm my nerves, Biff headed through the door. He walked straight past me to his office. I quickly grabbed the tickets from my purse and followed behind him.

"Uh sir, I have your tickets."

He turned around and snatched them from my hands. "Thanks."

"You're welco—." He slammed the door in my face.

Pompous bastard.

I went back to my desk and started my work for the day. Around two o'clock, the chime on the front door sounded. I peered up over my monitor and saw a delivery man headed toward my desk with an enormous bouquet of beautiful red roses.

"Hi, can I help you?"

"Yeah, I have a delivery for a..." he flipped through the pages on his clipboard, "Dorothy Meyers."

Really? Who the hell sent that bitch flowers?

A scowl covered my face as I looked at the flowers, then back at the delivery man.

"Look lady, does she work here or not? I gotta go."

"Yeah, she works here. Calm down John-Boy."

He shoved the clipboard at me. "You need to sign for 'em."

Just as I picked up my pen and was about to sign my John Hancock, Biff came out of his office.

"Ah! I see they arrived. Violet, I'll take care of that," he beamed, jerking the clipboard and pen from my hands. He scrawled on the paper, then handed the clipboard and some folded up money to the driver. "That's a little something for you, my good man!"

"Thanks!" he exclaimed, turning to leave.

Biff passed his nose through the flowers as he looked down at me sternly. I silent wished that a bee would have stung him. "Violet, please ring Dottie's desk and ask her to come up here so I can present these to her personally."

You have got to be shitting me!

Biff picked up the vase and disappeared into his office. I felt like I was in a bad dream. Was this really happening?

I reluctantly reached for my phone and started dialing her extension. As the line rang, the front door chimed again. I looked up and saw the flower guy headed toward me, so I hung up the phone.

"What now? Did you forget the box of candy?" I snarled.

"Uh, no, I forgot to deliver this. It was still on my truck."

I watched as he placed a slender purple glass vase with a single lavender rose on my desk.

"And who gets this one? The facilities guy?" I chided.

"According to my paperwork, it's for someone named Violet. There was no last name listed. But there is a card attached."

My heart almost stopped. Who was sending me flowers? I knew damn well it wasn't Biff. Maybe it was one of our clients thanking me for my help.

"Well, surprise, that would be me." My hands swirled in a quick circle, performing a little magic show. Tada.

He scratched his head as he handed me the paper to sign. "Oh, I get it, a violet for Violet," he cackled. I tried to see if there was any contact information in the sender box, but all it said was "private". I scribbled my name and handed the paper back to butthead.

"Enjoy!" he said, heading for the door.

As I racked my brain trying to figure out who would send me flowers, I removed the attached envelope and opened it, removing the small card tucked inside. The words were written in dark blue and simply stated "Rain, Rain, Go Away". Huh? What the hell did that mean? I was stumped. I smoothed my finger over the delicate petals. It was a beautiful piece of nature. Whoever sent it must either be a sweet person... or a homicidal maniac.

Biff's office door jerked opened, startling me.

"Violet!" he barked. "Did you call Dottie?"

"No sir, not yet. Someone was at the door and—"

"Excuses, excuses. Nevermind I'll do it myself!" He was at my desk in two steps and grabbed for the receiver.

"Dottie, It's Biff. Can you come up to the front for a few minutes? Thanks."

He hung up and looked down at my flower. Sarcastic laughter spilled from his lips. "What happened? He couldn't afford the other eleven stems?"

Just as I was about to respond, Dottie strolled up the hallway to my desk. She smiled at Biff while cautiously side-eyeing me. That's right bitch, you know better.

"You wanted to see me, Mr. Cartwell?"

"Yes Dottie I did. I wanted to thank you for getting me the VIP tickets to the Rancid Orchid concert. Buffy is going to be so surprised!"

I couldn't believe what I was hearing.

"You're welcome, sir! Really, it was no trouble. But I can't take all the credit."

That's right bitch, you better tell him how it really happened.

She shot a quick glance in my direction. "If it weren't for Rancid Orchid's people, we wouldn't have gotten them."

Biff put his arm around her shoulder. "You're too modest, Dot," he grinned. "I have a little token of my appreciation for you in my office."

Dot? That was it. I was gonna blast her ass again. I jumped up from my chair and walked behind them.

"Hey Dottie, why don't you tell Biff exactly who got the tickets for him?"

They both ignored me as they walked together into the office and shut the door. I felt my blood boil again. But before I let them get to me, I decided that I had had enough of The Cartwell Agency for one day. I logged off my computer, grabbed my purse, my precious flower, and headed for the door.

After squealing wheels out of the parking lot, I headed to the nail salon to treat myself to a mani-pedi. I just wanted to forget about the day. I was ready to relax and enjoy my weekend. I was feeling spicy, so I told the little Asian man who was helping me to paint both my fingers and toes red. And not just any shade of red, it was called "Do It To Me" red. After paying for my services, I walked next door to the liquor store and purchased a fresh bottle of Merlot.

"Hey Violet! How ya been?" asked Shay the store owner.

"Ok, busy with work. Ya know how that goes."

"Yeah, same shit different day."

We both laughed. Shay was a good guy. He'd been through two wives and three robberies, but still had his sense of humor. He had asked me out before, but I didn't look at him in that way. He was my friend and my happy-juice supplier.

"You got plans this weekend?"

I pretended to be thinking really hard. "Um... yeah, sit on my ass!"

Shay cracked up. "And see, that's why I love you, Violet."

I flashed him a quick smile. "Yeah, I know."

He rang up my purchase, then I paid him.

"Have a good one Shay."

"Bye baby, see you next time!"

I walked back to my car and headed home, ready to forget about Dottie and Biff, and ready to start my weekend.

CHAPTER FIVE

The morning sun spilled through my bedroom window and across the bed. I fully awakened, rolled over, and stretched. Ah, Saturday. I was ready to get my day of doing nothing started. I sat up and looked over at my nightstand, marveling at the little purple rose that graced it. It brought a smile to my face. I somehow needed to find out who sent it to me and thank them properly. I climbed out of bed and headed for the bathroom. After finishing, I went downstairs and fixed myself a bowl of peanut butter Cap'n Crunch, then planted my ass on the sofa to watch TV. Somewhere between Bugs Bunny and the midday matinee, I had dozed off. At almost two-thirty, the roar of my neighbor's lawn mower jolted me awake.

I got dressed and went outside to work in my in my garden. I loved gardening. When I was younger, I learned it from my grandmother. We spent a lot of time together and I will treasure it. She was like a second mother to me. Being among nature has always grounded me and soothed my soul. I gathered my tools and watering can and headed outside. I was very proud of my garden. My lush bouquet of lavender, coral and yellow impatiens was blooming beautifully. I was relishing in the warm rays of the afternoon sun and cheery songs of the crimson cardinals when the ringing of the telephone shattered my reverie. Ugh. I dashed into the house and grabbed for it.

"Hello?"

"Violet it's Biff."

Ah, hell… what did he want? I was NOT coming into work today.

"Yes sir, what's up?"

Biff's stern tone buzzed in my ear. "What's *up* is I didn't appreciate you leaving like you did yesterday. I don't know what kind of stunt you were trying to pull, or what has gotten into you lately, but you need to fix it ASAP!"

My merry mood was twisting into a pissed off one. "I'm sorry sir, but I wasn't feeling well so—"

"I don't care, Violet, just don't pull that shit again!"

"I won't sir," I lied.

"Good. Now look, the real reason I called is because I need a favor."

Oh, hell no. How was he going to chew me out, then ask for a favor? Especially after how this last favor turned out.

"A favor sir?" I reluctantly asked.

"Yes, my wife Buffy has come down with a stomach virus."

Too much caviar? "Sorry to hear that, sir." I didn't care. "But how does that affect me?"

"I need you to accompany me to the benefit tonight."

I paused for a moment. He couldn't be serious. "Why me? Why aren't you taking Dottie?" I sarcastically questioned. "After all, she was the one who got the tickets for you."

Annoyance crept into Biff's voice. "Look Violet, Dottie started her vacation, a much needed one I may add, and I need someone to go with me. This is a big chance for me to make some new contacts. It's the least you can do. I will be there at seven to pick you up."

Before I could respond, he hung up. The least I could do? Pfft. And here I thought he was actually going for the music. I should have known better. I sighed and rolled my eyes as I grabbed up my tools and can and headed back inside.

I fixed myself a sandwich, then headed upstairs to my bedroom. I laid the sandwich down on the nightstand, then started rummaging through my closet. Let's see, I was going to a benefit that also was a concert. A Rancid Orchid concert at that. If they were still the same Rancid Orchid, I remembered from those albums I had, I could have just went naked. But I was going with my boss and I guess, even though he was a jackass, I represented him, so I wanted to look nice. I settled on my long crimson satin gown. I took the dress out and laid it across the bed, then returned to the closet for my matching red Louis Vuitton heels.

As I reached up on the top shelf to grab my shoes, my hand brushed against a familiar box. I stopped and looked at it for a moment before deciding to pull it down. I took it over to the bed and sat down. My fingers lightly traced over the intricate design, down to the metal handles on each side. This black box contained my past. I had not opened it since I had moved here. It was who I used to be. It was what they judged me for. And I had tried to push that part of my life away and out of my mind. My fingers wandered back to the top of the box and circled around the lid. My eyes closed, and a huge sighed escaped me.

If only there was someone who would understand. Someone who could accept me for me.

I sat there for a while, wallowing in tarnished memories until my eyes misted over. I got up and put the box back in the closet. Right now, it was easier to just leave well enough alone. I grabbed my heels and shut the closet door.

Around six o'clock, I started getting ready. After taking my shower, I slipped on my red bra with matching lace panties and then my dress. I looked in the mirror. I must say I looked damn good for a woman of forty-five. I wasn't old, but damn if some days I didn't feel like I was eighty. I put my long hair up into an elegant bun, then applied my makeup. Just enough to highlight my light green eyes and some red lipstick. I glanced at my alarm clock. It said six forty-five. I applied some finishing touches, grabbed my heels, and headed downstairs. Sure enough, when seven o'clock rolled around, Biff was outside tooting the horn. I walked outside and headed toward the silver Aston Martin. He unlocked the passenger side door, and I carefully climbed in. He could have at least opened the door for me, but that was too much to ask.

"You look nice, Violet." His half-hearted remark vanished as fast as he expelled it.

"Thanks," I dryly replied.

He shifted the car into drive and we flew off into the night like two bats out of hell.

Let the fun begin.

CHAPTER SIX

The hour ride across town to the pavilion was silent and awkward. I would periodically look over at Biff, who was staring out the windshield, lost in thought. My mouth opened a few times to make some sort of small talk, but nothing would come out. So I focused my attention on the car. My eyes drank in the interior. The smooth black leather aircraft-like seats and grain wood were beautiful. Overall, it was a very nice and very expensive car. But I still loved my Firebird. You can never go wrong with the classics. Not a moment too soon, we finally arrived. Biff zoomed into the parking lot and a valet greeted us.

"Good evening, ma'am," the young kid announced as he held my door open and I stepped out of the car.

"Hello."

I waited on the curb and watched as he walked around to the driver's side and Biff tossed him the keys. "Be careful kid, that's my baby."

I rolled my eyes.

The kid nodded, and Biff walked over to me. He offered his arm, and I reluctantly linked mine with it.

"Shall we Violet?"

I plastered a phony smile on my face. "Sure."

We entered the large brick structure, and I gawked at the amount of people already there. Their wealthy, snobbish air flowed from them like a river. I felt like someone had sucked me into an episode of Lifestyles of The Rich and Famous. The poor and unfortunate were really gonna clean up tonight. Biff and I continued to walk around until he saw one of his colleagues.

"Look Violet, here's your ticket," he said, handing it to me and dropping my arm like a hot potato. "I'm going over to talk to Tom. See if you can find something to do. I'll come for you when it's time for the concert."

The hell? Was he embarrassed to be seen with me? And just what was I supposed to be doing? I shrugged and walked over to one of the hors d'oeuvre tables.

"Merlot," I told the attendant.

While I sipped, I looked around, noticing the décor of the event. The room was cast in a cobalt hue with peeks of silver here and there. Large glass vases full of beautiful multi-colored roses accentuated each table, nearly touching the overhead candelabras. The candlelight illuminating each table completed the look, filling the room with a relaxing ambiance. There was a small orchestra playing music in the corner. I wasn't sure what the name of the song was they were playing, but it was very soft and soothing. The whole affair was very nice and intimate. But all I could think about was how in the hell Rancid Orchid was going to fit in.

I finished my wine and quickly asked for a refill. Looking over at Biff, I watched as he threw his head back, roaring with laughter while he schmoozed with his friends. I sipped on my second glass of wine while

I enjoyed some of the cheese and cocktail shrimp that were offered. I may not have been having a lot of fun, but at least I was getting free booze, free food, and a concert out of the deal. As the last drop of wine slid over my tongue, the lights in the building flickered and there was an announcement over the PA system.

"Ladies and gentlemen, please take your seats. The show will begin in five minutes."

Should I wait for Biff, or should I go? I looked over at him again. He could have cared less where I was. So, I went to find my seat. I walked over to an usher and showed him my ticket. He told me to follow him and he lead me into the auditorium to row one, seat seven. Great, smack dab in front of everything.

I gingerly sat down, making myself as comfortable as possible in an evening gown, and looked up at the stage. The instruments were ready to take a pounding and the ten stacks of black Marshall amps sat ready to blow my eardrums. A rush of excitement shot through me. My mind wondered. What kind of show was this gonna be? How did these guys look after twenty years? And what about Grayson Maddox? I giggled to myself. "I hope he at least has pants on." This was definitely going to be interesting.

A few seconds later, I felt Biff sat down next to me. I turned to acknowledge him, but he ignored me. He was more interested in talking with the people in the row behind us. I turned back around to face the stage and begun wondering what songs they were going to sing. I hoped Grayson played his twelve-string guitar. There was just something sexy about the energy of a guitar solo that made me quiver. I hoped he was still the bad boy I remembered. In the middle of my musing, the place went completely black. Everyone started going bananas. The excitement was contagious, and the electricity buzzed through the air. The announcer's voice boomed once again over the PA system.

"Ladies and Gentlemen... are you ready to rock?... well it's the moment you've all been waiting for... tonight, The UIC Pavilion is proud to present... in a one night only appearance... those East Coast bad boys... RANCID ORCHID!"

Here we go!

CHAPTER SEVEN

"Helllloooo Chicago... are you ready to rock?" The roar of the audience became deafening. "That's good... cause I came to play." Man, that voice sounded so smooth... so sexy... so... familiar.

The red and gold curtain hiding the stage lifted and there, standing behind a microphone, draped with a cheetah print guitar, with his band, was bad boy extraordinaire Grayson Maddox.

But only it wasn't Grayson Maddox. It was Mr. Bertram.

OH SHIT!

That meant that Mr. Bertram was... and Grayson was... that meant that I...

The sudden feel of all the air rushing out of my body made me lightheaded. And the wine and shrimp I had consumed knocked at the back of my throat, begging my mouth to open up and expel them. I sat there in complete shock and awe. How was this possible?

"You ok Violet?" I heard Biff whisper in my ear. But I couldn't respond.

All I could do was stare. I probably looked like one of those cartoon characters whose eyes suddenly bugged out of their head. I didn't believe what I was seeing. He paused for a moment, then leaned into the microphone.

"Now I know y'all are expecting me to come out here and act like a wildman tonight..."

Whistles and cat calls bounced off the walls.

"But this is a special occasion and we're here for a good cause," he continued. "Don't worry, I'm still gonna please ya..." A slight smirk flashed on his face as he wiggled his eyebrows.

While the audience laughed and started clapping again, he swung back around, grabbed for his fingerboard and kicked off the show.

1... 2... 1-2-3-4! I saw her, and I knew she was the one... rock 'n roll beauty only out to have fun...

The place came to life with more applause. The song that washed over my ears was called *Dirty Rock Queen*. I hadn't heard that song in years. I was still in a daze. I thought about yesterday's encounter. That sexy man was right there, talking to me, standing ever so close. Those eyes... that mouth...

If I had only known.

My mind drifted back to the present as I watched him now. He was beautiful with his black zippered shirt and red leather pants. I watched his fingers glide across the strings of the guitar. The music coming from it, an extension of who he was. His brown mane swayed in the air surrounding him as he moved his head to the beat. At times, he would close his eyes and lose himself in his element. So was I. Something started stirring deep inside of me and I didn't know why, but I wanted to cry.

"Do you want ME?" he screamed into the microphone, pounding harder on his guitar. "Cause I want YOU!" He flicked his wrist and pointed toward my section. Right at me. "Said I want YOU!"

And right there, in that moment, I wanted him. Bad. Something was happening, and I didn't know what it was. He finished the song, and the audience cheered. He then went right into the next one. "Alright now, where are all my freaky ladies at?" his sexy voice cooed. "I'm lookin' for a hungry girl with a healthy appetite!" The women in the audience went wild.

I remember the day I met you
You were such a sexy thang
My heart went ping
And girl, you made my cock sing...

"Come on Chicago... I want ya to..." He paused and pointed the microphone at the audience.

"SUCK ON MY KNOB!" the audience screamed.

As Grayson sang the chorus, I felt Biff lean over and whisper against my ear again. "Is he singing about fellatio?" I jerked away from him and shook my head. And the winner of the dumbass of the year award is...

After finishing *Suck On My Knob*, they played *Fuck the Establishment*, *Just Shut Up* (I didn't know that one but it was now going to be my personal anthem) and *Fraudulent Messiah*. There was so much energy and sex appeal oozing from him. And the rest of the band were red hot too. After hitting the last note of Fraudulent Messiah, he throw off his guitar, kicked over the microphone stand and strutted off the stage. My eyes feasted on the sight of his tight ass and my tongue peeked out over my lips. Mmmm. The remaining members followed suit, and the audience went crazy as they started chanting. ORCHID... ORCHID. I still couldn't figure out how in the hell these upper crust frauds knew these songs.

A roadie appeared from the back and placed the microphone stand upright and collected the guitar. After what seemed like an eternity, the band reemerged, with Grayson bringing up the rear. The roadie handed him a gorgeous royal blue guitar, and he took his place at the front, absorbing the crowd's energy.

"Are you ready for round two?" he teased.

A rush of excitement traveled through my body at the sight. This was what I had been waiting for. As he eased his twelve-string across his lean body, a projection screen slowly lowered behind him. The screen came to life with a soft white glow, and a picture of Grayson with a large burly man appeared.

A lone spotlight now shone on him.

The audience quieted as he gazed upon them for a moment, then lowered his lips back to the microphone.

"On the second of this month, I lost someone very dear to me," he paused briefly, then continued. "This person was not only my bodyguard... he was my friend."

Another picture flashed on the screen. The heartbreak that consumed Grayson painted his face with sorrow, and the raw emotion that poured from him as he spoke made me want to cry with him.

"And... he was my family." His voice quivered momentarily before gaining in strength. "But I take comfort because I'm sure he's givin' the devil a run for his money!" He turned to face the screen behind him, raised his hand toward the heavens, and pointed. "Big Snake, this one's for you, brutha!"

His hand crashed down and smashed against his guitar strings. As soon as the d minor chord hit, the place erupted. He turned back around and stepped toward the microphone as another picture lit up the screen.

"Now Chicago... I know y'all know this song." He continued to play the opening riff to Pain in the Darkness. "I need ya to help me out... come on and let Snake hear ya."

If I had only known... that this was our last goodbye... I never would have hurt you... I never would have lied...

The audience joined in. "Pain in the darkness... pierces my black heart..."

A huge smile graced Grayson's lips. "That's right... pain... pain..."

When he got to the guitar solo, I looked around the room. It was a magical moment watching everyone joined in harmony. Hell, even Biff was singing. Yeah, guess he knew that song. It was the only song of theirs that commercial radio was allowed to play.

The handsome lead singer walked across the stage, threw his head back, and closed his eyes. I could see the faint trail of wetness that had stained his cheeks. His body swayed to the music that continued to flow from his soul, down through his fingertips and out of his Gibson. He poured every ounce of sorrow and energy he had into the song. My heart broke for him. When the song returned to the chorus, he opened his eyes and looked down.

Then it happened. Amber eyes locked with green.

At that moment, only two people existed in the world. It seemed like a thousand years before he finally looked away. I felt my heart stop. He took a step back and another quick glance, then went back to the microphone.

"Come on, everybody help me out... get on your feet... raise your hands if you know what I'm talkin' bout... pain in the darkness."

The audience grew louder. Everyone was on their feet, waving their arms. He started playing his guitar again and, as he got to the end of the song, he slowed down. "The pain will always pierce my heart, Big Snake. Thank you Chicago! We love you all! Goodnight!" And with that, he hit the last note, and the spotlight went out. The place was in hysterics. The curtain came down, and the houselights went up. I had never been so moved in my whole life.

"Are you crying Violet?" Biff asked, looking at me, perplexed.

I sniffed. "No sir, it's just my allergies." I don't think he believed me, and I really didn't care.

I picked up my purse and followed behind him. "Violet, would you like to accompany me to the VIP party? Or shall I take you home?"

I weighed my options. I wanted to go just to see what it would be like. And Biff would probably just leave me again, anyway. But what would I do if I actually ran into HIM? I really wasn't looking forward to that interaction. Then again, after that emotional performance, he probably wanted to be alone. I let out a shaky breath and made my decision.

"I'll go with you, sir."

I followed Biff out of the auditorium and into the hallway, where we once again linked arms. We walked a few feet to a corridor that had a sign stating VIP Guests Only. Biff and I showed our tickets to the balding, stiff lipped man in the tuxedo and he unhooked the black velvet rope, letting us through.

Here goes nothing.

CHAPTER EIGHT

We entered the VIP lounge and joined a group of about forty people. Once again, shades of blue adorned everything. I get it now. Blue must be Grayson's favorite color. Against two of the walls sat white plush-looking sofas and a couple of huge, black, throne-like chairs. And along the other two were long buffet tables decorated with silver tablecloths, hosting large gold platters filled with lobster tails, caviar and filet mignon. A flowing Champaign fountain completed the elegant ensemble. Our lighting was being provided by a glass chandelier the size of Montana and a DJ provided the tunes playing in the background. There was a door in the far back corner of the room labeled *Private—GM*. I assumed it was Grayson's dressing room. It was a given that he always had a separate room from the rest of the band. My brain hoped that he had already left for the evening and wasn't hiding in there. But my body wanted to barge in there, lock the door, and fuck his brains out.

Biff had left me once again to go make new friends, so I walked over to one of the buffet tables. I reached for one of the small trident forks, took a piece of steak, and popped it in my mouth. It was so tender and moist. As I continued nibbling on the small delicacy, the attendant poured a large flute of Champaign and handed it to me. I really didn't mind being alone. It was better than pretending to be something that I wasn't, unlike Biff. I finished my steak and continued sipping on my drink as the DJ announced the next song.

"Alright everyone, we're gonna slow it down. I want all you lovers out there to pull your significant other close as we take it back to '79 with some Earth, Wind & Fire."

The light in the room dimmed as *"After the Love Has Gone"* started playing and I watched all the couples dance. The alcohol traveling through my body was taking effect, and I was feeling tipsy. I closed my eyes and my body started swaying as I got lost in the song.

I was so lost in my lonely world that I never felt the two hands that had snaked around my waist or the body that was now swaying with mine. I leaned back and pressed myself into the warmness behind me. It felt so good.

"That's one of my favorites too," a deep baritone breathed in my ear.

I suddenly stopped dancing. It was like someone had poured ice water over my head. I knew that voice this time. It was HIM. He had caught me off guard. And although I didn't show it on the outside, I was still reeling from what I had just experienced. I felt like a mouse caught in a trap. I jerked and pulled myself loose from his grip, spinning around.

"Just what do you think you're doing?"

He laughed a little as he threw up his hands. "Calm down, baby. I wasn't tryin' anything."

My eyes bore into his. "Baby? I ain't your baby!"

"Well, it's nice to see you again too, Miss Violet."

I took one last gulp of my Champaign and slammed the delicate glass on the table. "Well, Mr. Maddox, or should I call you Bertram? I don't know if I'm as happy to see you!"

He frowned in puzzlement.

"Although I appreciate what you did for me, you could have at least told me who you were the other night," I spat, turning to walk away. The noise level in the room quickly died down as all eyes darted in our direction.

"Violet wait..."

He grabbed my arm and stopped me. I turned to face him. Don't look in his eyes... don't look in his eyes. But I did. He had the same sincere look he had when we met the other night. But the look in his eyes also told me I couldn't ignore him. His thumb lightly skimmed over my upper arm, causing little waves of pleasure.

"Come with me."

I jerked out of his grip and folded my arms together. "I'm not going anywhere with you!"

"Yes, you are!"

And just when did he become my boss?

I huffed at him and threw my hands up in the air. "Fine!"

He grasped my hand and quickly intertwined our fingers, leading me through the sea of gawking onlookers to the room that said *Private —GM*. He opened the door and allowed me to enter first. At least he seemed like a gentleman. It was a stark contrast to the room we just left. Pictures and writings from previous performers decorated the pale walls. There was a small table with a mirror, a make-up chair, a taupe colored loveseat with many tears and a long green army cot. So much for the star treatment. The entire room was lit by candlelight. I guess there wasn't enough left in the budget after buying the chandelier. He shut the door and my body slightly flinched at the sound of the lock being applied. He walked over to the loveseat and sat down, patting the space next to him.

"Come, sit with me."

I stared at him. There was no way in hell I was going near him again.

"Aww, c'mon. I don't bite… unless that's what you want."

I hesitated for what seemed like an eternity before apprehensively walking over to fill the empty space. Awkward tension saturated the room. The alcohol I had drank and my nerves were getting the best of me. I felt the beginnings of a tremble stirring in my body.

The handsome lead singer studied my face. "If you don't mind me saying… you look beautiful," he finally said, breaking the ice. "Red is a lovely color on you."

A blush graced my face, and my eyes darted to the floor. "Thank you."

"You look better than the last time I saw you," he chuckled.

I continued staring at the worn carpeted floor, silently wishing it would open up and swallow me whole.

"Look, I'm sorry I didn't tell you who I was the other night. It's just that…"

I returned my eyes to his face. "It's just what?"

He leaned back and smoothed a large hand through his long tresses. "It's just that at first I thought you were acting like you didn't know who I was," he sighed. "But as we kept talking, I realized you really didn't."

I flashed him a slight, knowing smile. "And I'm sorry I didn't know who you were. I mean, I know who you are. I have some of your records, but they're the first ones you ever made. I really haven't kept up with you."

A look of pain flashed across his face.

"I'm sorry Mr. Maddox... uh... Bertram... that came out wrong... I didn't mean—"

He put his hand up to stop me and shook his head. "No, it's ok. Please don't feel bad." A long breath he seemed to have been holding escaped his lungs. "Actually, it was kinda refreshing to find someone who wasn't all star-struck."

He gently reached for my hand and cradled it in his own. "And please... just call me Grayson."

His touch was burning up my porcelain skin. I swallowed hard. "Ok... Grayson. I'm sorry about your friend. He must have meant a lot to you."

"Thank you. And yes, he did."

That now familiar silence deafened the room again as his warm amber orbs gazed into my green ones. I felt a wave of heat wash over my whole body. His scent, a mixture of light oak, musk, and sweat, intoxicated my nose. And the way the candlelight illuminated his features was breathtaking. I imagined how his naked body would look bathed in the soft glow. My eyes left his and skimmed downward, across the solidness of his tight t-shirt. I wanted to reach out and run my hands across it, play with the zippers. But even more so, I wanted to rip off that shirt and brand his chest with my kisses. I continued my observation, drinking in the sight of his slightly soft abdomen before coming to rest on the secret bulge waiting to be revealed inside those painted-on red pants. For a man in his fifties, he was still a looker. A sudden rush of wetness coated my lace panties. What was this man doing to me?

"Violet..."

I loved the way my name rolled off his tongue and across his pink, pouty lips. I suddenly wanted to hear him moan it as I swallowed his cock.

My gaze slowly returned to his. "Yes Grayson?"

He took a deep breath. "I know this might sound crazy... but have you ever felt an instant connection to someone you just met?"

It was like he was reading my mind. "Honestly... no. But now," I paused for a moment, "I think I have."

His eyes continued gazing into mine as he contemplated his next move. He let go of my hand and brought his own up to my face, gently cupping my cheek. My eyes fluttered shut, and I turned into his palm, relishing in the feeling of his touch. The next thing I knew, his hot breath was whispering against my ear.

"I'm glad... because I want to know everything about you."

As my eyes peeked open, a pair of soft lips began pecking at mine. He had caught me. I couldn't escape. I didn't want to escape. The kiss increased in intensity before he tore away and started blazing a wet trail down the arch of my neck. I re-closed my eyes and let the feeling overtake me.

"I wanna know how you taste," he murmured against my skin as his firm hand bunched up the hem of my dress and slid underneath, inching its way up my thigh, grabbing for my satin panties.

His exquisite touch was igniting a fire inside of me. I was ready to come right there. I leaned back against the loveseat and sighed in ecstasy.

"Uh... fuck."

His smooth lips continued their sweet torture on my neck before moving across the dip of my collarbone, down to my chest. His tongue peeked out and skimmed the swells of my large breasts. "And I wanna know," he purred, opening his mouth, drawing my left breast into it, sucking on it, "what you sound like when I make you come." His teeth barred down on my nipple and I moaned. "Grayson..."

I couldn't believe this was really happening. I never wanted this feeling to end. Time was at a standstill. We were the only two people in the world at the moment. My mind was delirious with desire and my willpower was fading fast. I entangled my hands in his soft, flowing hair as he moved forward and gently lowered his body onto mine. His hand snaked around to the back of my dress and lowered the zipper. "You can't run away now baby... you're all mi—"

A sudden pounding on the door combined with loud shouting shattered our interlude.

"Just let me in there! She's my secretary!" I knew exactly who that voice belonged to. The pounding at the door continued.

"Shit! Sorry, baby," Grayson soothed as his lips left my body and he quickly climbed off me. "Just a minute," he called out, his pissed off tone flavoring his voice. He fixed my zipper and waited until I had composed myself before he opened it. An enormous man in a black dress shirt and pants waited on the other side.

"Sorry to interrupt boss, but this jackass... I mean, guy, claims that he is looking for some girl named Violet and says he thinks she is in here."

"It's cool," Grayson plainly stated as he turned around to look at me before moving to the side, out of the doorway. I gave a slight wave to Biff, who was standing there fuming.

"For chrissakes there you are! I've been looking everywhere for you. I hope you had fun because I'm ready to go!"

I glared at Biff, then looked at Grayson. Neither man was smiling.

"Yes sir, I'm sorry," I mumbled, jumping up from the loveseat, smoothing out my dress.

Grayson looked at me, then moved back to the open door, getting in Biff's face. "The name's Grayson Maddox. And you are?"

Biff looked at him like he had three heads. "I'm Biff Cartwell. And I know who the hell you are. My wife and I are big fans," he bullshitted, grabbing Grayson's hand and shaking it. "I apologize for my assistant's behavior this evening. Sometimes she just doesn't know what to do with herself."

Grayson jerked his hand out of Biff's and twisted his face in anger. "Apologize? For what? She has done nothing wrong. Look, I brought her here so we could talk. Is there a problem with that?"

Biff backed away. "No," he huffed, "but I'm ready to leave and I have to haul her ass back home. So come on Violet, let's go!"

Grayson took a step forward. "Well, if you need to go, then go! I'll make sure she gets home safely."

Biff's roar of laughter shook the walls. "Sure Bon Jovi, whatever you say. Why don't you just mind your own business and go back to playing your gee-tar!"

Grayson was livid. "Who the fuck you callin' Bon Jovi?" He was ready to pounce. "And for *your* information, she is my business!"

My heart leaped at the sudden protectiveness he was showing towards me. But things were escalating quickly, and I knew Biff was about to get his ass beat. Which was fine with me because he deserved it, but I didn't want Grayson to get in trouble. I walked over to the door and lightly touched his arm as I turned to face him. "That won't be necessary, but thank you for the offer. I've had a really nice evening. I will never forget it."

A new emotion now filled me... sadness.

"Just remember what I told you," he gently whispered as he grabbed my hand and placed a kiss on it. "Until next time Miss Violet."

My eyes burned with tears at the thought of never seeing him again. "Until then, Mr. Maddox," my voice quivered.

"I'm waiting, Violet!" Biff called as he stormed away.

I reluctantly turned away from the beautiful man before me and followed behind Biff. I wanted to look back at his face one last time, sear his image to my memory, but I couldn't bring myself to do it. So, I walked out of the building and out of his life.

The ride home was once again silent. I didn't dare say anything to Biff because he was fuming. We reached my driveway, and I had barely stepped out of the car and shut the door when he sped off into the night. Monday was not something I was looking forward to. After trudging to the front door, I headed upstairs and threw myself across the bed. I didn't know if it was all the alcohol I had consumed or if it was my darkened heart beating once again, but my tears came. And this time, I let every one of them fall. I let them fall throughout the night until sleep finally claimed me.

CHAPTER NINE

Sometime the next morning, I awoke to the sound of pouring rain. I untangled myself from the comforter and climbed out of bed. My heels had fallen off onto the floor during the night and my dress was beyond wrinkled. My hair had come loose and half of it was hanging in my face. There was a dull ache knocking at my temples and my eyes were red and puffy. But all of that didn't compare to the pain that was searing my heart. I didn't know why I was so emotional. It had been so long since I even looked at a man. My heart had been so badly broken that I wanted nothing to do with the male species. I had perfected the wall I had built around myself and vowed not to let anyone in.

Then along came Grayson Maddox with a bulldozer.

I didn't care that he was a famous rock star. The man behind the facade intrigued me. There had to be more to him than just his music and bad boy reputation. Even though we had just met, the thought of never seeing or talking to him again broke my heart. I stripped out of my dress and let down the rest of my hair. I went into the bathroom, grabbed two Tylenol from the medicine cabinet and washed them down with a nice, cool glass of water. Reaching for the shower knob, I turned it to a relaxing temperature and climbed in. I just wanted to wash the remnants of last night, and the pain, away.

After finishing my shower, I slipped on my pajamas and headed to the kitchen to scrounge for nourishment. I had no appetite, but I ended up fixing some toast with butter and jelly and a glass of orange juice. I planted myself on the couch and turned on the TV. There really isn't much to choose from on Sunday mornings. I flipped through the channels, finally landing on VH1. I watched some videos and half-heartedly sang along as I finished my breakfast. Gulping down the last drop of my juice, I returned to the kitchen for a refill. As I reached in the refrigerator for the bottle, I heard the announcer's voice booming from the living room.

Coming up next on VH1... we're gonna paint the day black and red with those East Coast bad boys Rancid Orchid! Join us for a two-hour video block, then stick around for a rare showing of the banned concert Rancid Orchid Live at MSG. Stay cool and stay tuned!

I damn near dropped the bottle and my glass on the floor. After slamming the refrigerator shut, I set the bottle and glass on the counter, then ran back into the living room. There he was, in all his glory, oozing sweat and sex all over my TV screen. I flopped down on the couch and sighed. This was all I had now—videos, movies and records. I promised myself right then and there to buy every album they ever made. All I could do was watch. I didn't want to miss one minute. When the commercials came on, I wouldn't change the channel. I had forgotten how good their music really was. At the end of the concert, Grayson climbed on top of the amps, played a kick-ass guitar solo, then jumped down and obliterated his guitar into a million fragments. It was awesome!

A sudden knock on my front door jolted me back to reality. Who the hell was that?

The credits started rolling, so I went to find out. I opened the door and there was nobody there. Hmm... damn neighborhood kids. I peeked out and looked around. Nothing. As I went to close the door, I noticed something taped to it. It was an envelope that said *Read Me* on the front. That's funny, I paid all my bills. Well, at least I thought I did.

I pulled it off, brought it inside, and sat back down on the couch. As I carefully opened the envelope, a familiar scent of musk wafted past my nose. I reached in and my fingers removed the most delicate piece of beige parchment paper. As I opened it, purple flower petals gently floated into my lap. At that moment, I realized that I'd never thanked him for the first flower he gave me. Red ink revealed the contents of the note.

My Dearest Violet,
I meant every word of what I said when I told you we're connected. I can see it in your eyes. It is the reflection of how I also feel. There is no time that can steal, or space that can separate, what is destined to be.
Until we meet again...
~GM

Both my eyes, and my heart, were in shock. How did this letter get here? Did he put it there? How did he know where I lived? My brain went into overdrive trying to figure out the answers to these questions. I had to take a deep breath to keep from hyperventilating. Oh shit! Was he outside? I jumped up from the couch and ran into the coffee table as I sprinted for the door. "Ouch! Damn it!" I yelled, grabbing at my leg as I jerked it opened and ran outside, down the sidewalk.

"Grayson?" I called out, looking up and down the street, but not seeing anyone. "Grayson? Are you here?"

I was sure my neighbors thought I was some kind of loon walking around in the rain, calling for Grayson when they knew I didn't have any pets. I took one last look around, then went back inside.

I fell back down on the couch in defeat. My heart had gone from zero, leaped to a thousand, then crashed back to zero all in a span of five minutes. I was drained. The little white envelope fell to the floor as I picked up the letter and walked into the kitchen. I grabbed my fresh bottle of Merlot from the cabinet and headed upstairs. I climbed back into bed, threw the covers over my body, cracked opened the wine and downed a huge gulp. The dam holding back my tears broke, and they started flowing like a raging river. I reread the letter repeatedly as my fingers traced over every word. His words. Turning my head, I spied my little purple rose and the card next to it. How did he know it was my favorite color? It seemed I had more questions that I would ever have answers. Another gulp of dark fruit and herbal notes slid down my throat.

Oh, Grayson, where are you tonight?

I tucked the card inside the letter, folded it up, and placed it under my pillow. My gloomy thoughts turned to those of Grayson as my wet eyes slowly closed. As I drifted off to sleep, I could see his smiling face in my mind. It brought a smile to my own.

CHAPTER TEN

Monday morning arrived in all its glory. I woke up earlier than usual, got dressed, and prepared myself mentally for the day that was ahead of me. I still had little appetite, so I skipped breakfast and headed off to meet my fate. Arriving at work early, I was the first person there. Usually, I have to park in the parking lot, but today I snagged a spot in the parking garage. I made my way inside the old brick structure and climbed into an elevator. A minute later, the door chime dinged as I entered the office. Ah, hell sweet hell. I headed straight to the break-room and put on a fresh pot of coffee.

As I waited, I went to my desk and logged onto my computer. I sat my purse on my lap and opened it. Reaching inside, I pulled out the letter and re-read it, smoothing my fingers across it yet again. My mind was confused, but my heart felt full. The smell of Colombian dark roast soon tickled my nose, so I returned the letter and went to pour myself a cup. As I relished in the hot soothing beverage, my co-workers filed in like cattle headed off to slaughter. The only good thing about this week was the fact that Dottie was on vacation. I could actually work in peace. I sat back down and immersed myself in today's files. At a half-past nine, Biff graced the office with his presence.

I lowered my head to avoid him. "Good morning, sir."

He stormed past me so fast I swear I caught a cold from the updraft.

"My office NOW Deveraux!"

As much as I had tried to prepare for this moment, I still wasn't ready when it came. I could hear the whispers and feel the eyes staring at me as I slowly entered Biff's office and closed the door. I took a seat in the old wooden chair in front of his desk, looked up at him, and swallowed hard. I felt like I just got called into the principal's office.

"You wanted to see me, sir?"

Biff's baby blues glowered at me before he finally answered. "Yes, Violet, I did. I wanted to talk to you about the other night."

"What about the other night, sir?" I quietly asked, knowing damn well what he meant.

He clasped his enormous hands together behind his head and leaned back in his leather chair. The squeak of the bolts echoed throughout the room.

"Well... Violet... I don't even know where to begin. Should I start with the fact that you disappeared without telling me where you were going... or..." he paused for a split second, "the fact that I caught you being a whore with Grayson Maddox? Is that what you are now? Of all people Violet! Are you a groupie?"

A whore? A groupie? What the fuck was wrong with him? I tried reasoning with him. "With all due respect, sir, I'm not a whore and I wasn't being a groupie. All we were doing was talking."

Biff roared with a mock laugh. "Talking? Is that what it's called nowadays?"

My temper was rearing its ugly head, but I kept it under control. I felt like I was being interrogated by the FBI. "Sir, although you were nice enough to bring me with you to the benefit, you told me to find something to do while you made new contacts. Grayson came to me. He even told you that himself."

"You're damn right I was nice enough to let you take Buffy's place! And that's how you repay me? Do you know how much you embarrassed me? Do you think those people will want to do business after seeing me drag my assistant out of Grayson Maddox's dressing room? Trust me, Violet, that washed-up has-been, has had his fair share of women. You aren't THAT special. Yeah, he said he brought you there, but I think it's bullshit!"

I rose from my chair and stood my ground. "It's the truth, sir!"

Biff leaned forward, unlocked his hands and slammed them down on his desk like two large boulders. "Don't get an attitude with me, Violet! I've been very patient with you for a long time now."

My insides started shaking. I had a bad feeling about what was getting ready to happen. "I don't have an attitude with you."

"Yes, you do. I have put up with a lot of things you've done and overlooked them. But I think this might be the final straw. NOBODY messes with Biff Cartwell's money!"

Biff jumped out of his chair and started pacing around the room like a caged tiger. "Violet, I'm pissed. In fact, I'm beyond pissed."

This was it. My career was over. I was going to have to move into the box that my belongings were soon going to be packed in.

When he stopped, his six-four frame was looming over me. "But, because I'm the nice guy that I am, I've decided not to fire you over this fiasco."

Really? Nice guy? Shit was getting deep real fast. I felt some relief knowing that I wouldn't lose my job. Then he finished.

"However, I am going to suspend you for two weeks without pay until you can get your shit together. Your suspension starts right now."

Two weeks? Was he serious? This wasn't fair. "But sir!" I protested.

"Do you want to try for a month? My decision is final, Violet." Biff waved his hand in front of my face. "Now leave my presence before I change my mind!"

I jumped up from the chair, gathered up what pride I had left, and slammed the door behind me. I hoped he got a good look at my ass because he can kiss it! After logging off my computer, I grabbed my purse, threw open the reception door and stormed down the hallway to the ladies' room.

It was only ten o'clock.

Slinking into the farthest stall, I locked the door and let my tears flow like a waterfall. I was so angry I couldn't stop shaking. I had done nothing wrong and yet everything was my fault. It always was. What was I going to do now? Two weeks off with no pay. I had some savings stashed away. Hopefully, it would tie me over. A quick flash ran through my mind of my former life. I couldn't go back to it, no matter how desperate I was. Sure the money was good but...

The sound of someone coming into the bathroom caused me to quiet my sobs. I unrolled some toilet paper, dried my eyes, and blew my nose. I put on my game face and pulled myself together before anyone saw me. Scurrying back out into the hallway, I jumped into the first available elevator.

I reached the first floor and headed to the parking garage. I didn't know where to go or what to do. My heels clicked across the pavement as I fumbled through my purse, looking for my keys. I finally found them, pulled them out, and threw them on the ground. Shit!

I bent down to pick them up and thought I saw something out of the corner of my eye. I didn't pay any attention to it and kept walking until I heard a noise. It was a low whistle. I felt sorry for whoever this was because the mood I was in was a dangerous one. The whistle sounded again. I put my keys back in my purse, turned around and headed in the whistler's direction to give them a piece of my mind.

"Look here, you sorry son of a bitch, I don't need—"

My feet stopped dead in their tracks. The sight I held before me nearly made my heart flatline. Sitting perched on the hood of a dark jade Jaguar, in all his glory, was Grayson.

CHAPTER ELEVEN

"What don't you need, Violet?" his deep baritone questioned. He reached out toward me and curled his index finger. "Come here..." I willed my feet to break free from the invisible glue holding them and hesitantly moved over to the car. Was he really here? Or had my mind finally checked out? He swung his long jean-covered legs over the side, pushed himself off the glossy paint, and sauntered over to stand in front of me. The sound of his boots echoed off the concrete slabs of the garage.

"How did you—?"

"Shh... it ain't time for all those questions," he cooed, placing a long finger to my lips. "And besides, I have my ways."

My emotional eyes met his, and his hands swiftly reached for my face. "You've been crying." Concern flavored his words as he gently wiped away my tears with his thumbs.

I nodded and lowered my head.

"Why are you cryin', baby?"

A shaky breath left my body, and the waterworks started again.

"Damn it Violet! I wanna know who did this," Grayson huffed, his face flushing with anger with each passing second. His large hands grabbed mine and brought them to his chest. "Tell me baby, cause I'm gonna kick their ass!"

My voice cracked as I looked up at him. "My boss… Biff."

A low growl rumbled deep in his chest, rising to his throat. "That snobbish bastard? I should've known! Especially after the way he treated you the other night… and after what he said to me… I should have beat his ass right then and there!"

A light chuckle wafted over my lips as he lightly skimmed the backs of my hands with his calloused thumbs. "What happened?"

I inhaled deeply. "Well, he accused me of being a whore… a groupie, actually. I told him what really happened between us the other night and he didn't believe me. He said that because of my behavior, I cost him money and embarrassed him."

A splash of red painted the middle-aged rocker's face. "The fuck? A groupie? All we were doin' was talkin'. Ok, maybe we were doin' more than that, but that's none of his fuckin' business!"

"I know. And…" I steeled my nerves for his reaction at what I was about to say, "he suspended me."

Grayson Maddox was more than mad. He was livid. He dropped my hands and feverishly paced back and forth. "Whaddya mean he suspended you? How did *you* cost him money? That contrary motherfucker probably has more money than I do!"

I tried to hold back for fear that he would explode and just make good on his promise to kick Biff's ass. "He said he had to drag me out of your dressing room and I embarrassed him in front of all the contacts he had just made."

Grayson stopped momentarily and stared at me with bated breath. "I see... why do I feel like there's more to it?"

I couldn't lie to him. So, I lowered the boom. "The suspension is for two weeks... and it's without pay."

The swift blur and crunch of a fist connecting with concrete made me jump. "That's bullshit, Violet, and he knows it! He can't do that!" Grayson shook his head and sucked his teeth, nursing his quickly bruising hand. "Man... he better pray that we're never alone again in the same room!"

"Well, he did." My eyes misted over again. "And I don't know what I'm gonna do..."

Grayson moved to stand in front of me, enveloped my shaking body in his powerful arms, and I laid my head on his shoulder. "It's gonna be alright mama," he soothed, stroking his hands up and down my back. At that moment, I had never felt so safe. I knew he would never let anyone hurt me. I could have stayed in his arms forever. My sobs soon turned to sniffles and after a few more sniffs, I gently pulled away from him. "Thank you."

He smiled at me, then leaned in and softly pecked my lips. As he pulled back, we looked at each other. The cool October air had turned into an August sizzle. There was no more denying the desire and want between us. He leaned in for another kiss, but this time there was no peck. There was only need. His soft lips crashed against mine with such force that it almost toppled me over. The smooth velvet of his tongue hungrily knocked for entry and my pink-colored pucker gladly surrendered. He tasted like cool mint. We devoured each other like it was our last day on Earth. With every moan that escaped us, my willpower dissolved a little more. Our tongues mixed and mingled like two dancing cobras, fighting for dominance. He crushed my bottom lip between his pearly whites and gently bit down. The electrifying tingle shook my whole body.

This was too good to be true. He was too good to be true. Too good for me.

I put my hands on his solid chest and pushed him away with all my might.

"I can't do this."

Grayson looked at me as he tried to catch his breath. His face was flush and his desire laden eyes swam with confusion. "What's wrong?"

My heart and eyes pleaded one thing, but the reality swirling in my brain said another. All I could do was look at him. I'm sorry. Before I knew it, my legs were carrying me in the opposite direction.

"Violet! Where the hell you goin'?"

My heels clicked through the garage as I walked faster. Grayson's own boots echoed on the concrete right behind me. He was yelling now. "Damn it Violet, answer me!"

I reached my Firebird, threw open the clutch on my Coach bag, and grabbed the keys. I fumbled with the little piece of metal, trying to stick it in the door, but my damn fingers wouldn't stop shaking. On about the fourth try, I finally got the key in the lock and turned it. That's when I felt him come up behind me. His fast hands grabbed my waist and spun me around. Hazel eyes once again locked with emerald.

"What are you running from?" he said, searching my face for some kind of answer. The sound of our heavy breathing filled the surrounding space. He deserved an honest answer. I just didn't know if I wanted to give it. But as those damn piercing eyes continued to bore into mine, looking past me and into my soul, the answer left my lips.

"This. I'm afraid of this."

Grayson leaned his head back as he continued to study me. "Why?" sincerity flavored his words. "I've already told you how I feel."

I looked at him, then darted my gaze. "Yes Grayson, I know. But you need to understand... there are things about me... dark things. And I.... I don't want to hurt you."

I needed to get out of there, and fast. As much as I wanted to be with him, he didn't deserve someone like me. He would never understand the things that I had done... or the things I still craved. I turned back around and reached for the door handle. I felt him move closer to me.

"Dark things? Let me tell you about dark things baby..."

The words formed by his hot, minty breath tickled my ear, while his salt and pepper goatee scratched against the soft skin of my cheek. A small flame was igniting in the fleshy spot between my legs as he pressed his solid body up against mine.

"Babygirl, I've lived through some shit. So whatever your story is, trust me, I will understand. But... if you're talkin' about something sexual," his voice deepened from baritone to bass, and I could have sworn there was a hint of danger mixed in it, "mmm... baby... there ain't nothin' darker than *my* fantasies."

His firm body pressed tighter against mine, and he planted both hands on either side of me, on top of the car. I was now pinned between the frame and the bulging hardness that was pressing into my ass.

"You feel that?" he whispered, moving his right hand to sweep my long chestnut locks to the side, kissing my neck. "That, Miss Violet, is what you do to me. It's been there since the first time I saw you."

My heartbeat became erratic, my breaths hitched and the flame between my legs was turning into a raging inferno. I squeezed my thighs together as hard as I could to squelch the throbbing. It didn't help.

"Do you remember that day?"

I nodded.

"You made me stand there and look at you... dripping wet... in that tiny skirt... with your perfect breasts and succulent nipples teasing me through that lavender blouse... and what about those knee-high stiletto boots hmm... black suede with metal buckles... those come fuck me boots?"

My body sighed in ecstasy as he continued his assault on my neck and his hand inched its way around my waist. Without even realizing what was happening, my feet led me from the side of the car to the front of it. I silently thanked God that I had parked next to a secluded wall.

"You're a bad girl, Violet," he teased as he slowly, yet forcefully, bent me over the hood. "I bet you're wet right now."

My mind tried to comprehend what was happening as he ran his hands down my back. Leaving one perched on my ass, the other one reached for the hem of my skirt.

"Wha... what... are you doing?"

His calloused fingers eased their way underneath and crept up my thigh, reaching for the smooth band of my black lace panties. In one fell swoop, they were down around my ankles.

"Making it all better sweetness..."

My emerald orbs rolled to the back of my head as he smoothed across the small black curls of my pussy, sneaking between my folds. He methodically stroked me, up and down, around in a circle, pinching at my clit.

"I was right... you're dripping."

One of his fingers plunged deep into my core and I almost came. "You're so tight baby... how long has it been?"

I spread my legs wider and flattened myself against the freshly waxed metal hood, bending my fingertips to keep my nails from scratching the shiny dark green paint. He continued his steady rhythm, joining another finger with the first one, stretching me as his free hand pushed my skirt all the way up. He rubbed my bare ass before punishing it with a loud smack.

"You like that?"

Oh God, how I did. All I could do was whimper like a puppy.

"Aww what's the matter... *SMACK*... cat got your tongue?"

SMACK

"Tell me Violet... *SMACK*... what is your dark secret?"

My body was going to combust into flames and my brain could no longer form a complete thought. At that point, I would have given him my soul.

"I... use... use to..."

A low laugh rose from the depths of his chest as he continued finger-fucking me. "That's not the answer I'm looking for."

SMACK

"Come on now... just be a good girl and tell me... I promise daddy will make it all better if you do."

I was panting now and I could feel a hot coil tightening in my lower stomach. Yes, he could be my daddy. I would even make him my master. He was awakening things in me I had kept hidden for so long. He suddenly pulled his fingers out and I damn near cried at the loss of contact.

"DAMN IT VIOLET... NOW!"

Time and space no longer existed. My mind and my body swirled in an oblivion as they pleaded for him to grant me sweet release. I couldn't take it anymore.

"I USED TO BE A DOMINATRIX!"

And with that declaration, my ache was relieved as his warm tongue filled my core. He lapped at my pussy and nibbled on my clit like a famished man presented with a cornucopia of food.

"Ahhh... fuck... go... faster!"

He increased the pace as he continued his sweet torture. The ferocity of his actions pushed me further up onto the hood until my feet barely touched the ground. My orgasm was growing and there would be nothing I could do to stop it.

"Mmmm..." I felt him murmur against my wet, pink hole.

My heart thundered against my rib cage as I threw my head back in wild abandonment. My body was on the verge of breaking out into a sweat. I was so close... just a few... more... strokes... and...

"COME!" Grayson forcefully commanded with one last stroke.

The kaleidoscope of color bursting forth momentarily blinded me as I collapsed on the car, feeling my walls spasm and my juices flow. After drinking every drop, Grayson stood up and hovered over my body, leaning against my ear. "So sweet... just like honey."

As my breathing returned to normal, he helped me off of the car. He reached down and lifted my legs one by one, smoothing my panties over my heels. He then folded them up and put them in his pocket. I looked at him with a smirky grin.

"My souvenir," he stated matter-of-factly.

As I smoothed out my skirt and top, he walked over and took my hands in his.

"Well, I was supposed to leave for Seattle in a few hours. But something has changed my mind."

"Oh really? And just what might that be?"

He closed the distance between us and placed his lips on mine. The faint taste of my essence covered them. After a few moments, we pulled apart.

"I'm going to leave you my card. It has my hotel information on it. I want to see you again, Violet. Don't keep me waiting."

He pulled a card from his pocket and placed in my hand as he graced it with a soft kiss.

I watched him walk away, and soon the Jaguar was roaring out of the garage.

I hopped in my Firebird and sat for a while, trying to comprehend what had just happened.

What was I gonna do now?

CHAPTER TWELVE

I sat in my car and tapped the little white card against the steering wheel. Things had definitely taken an unexpected turn. He had dominated the dominatrix. I could still feel him... his touch... his tongue. A small aftershock rumbled between my legs. I read the card again. The Langham Hotel – Infinity Suite – Twelfth Floor. I closed my eyes and leaned back against the headrest, sighing. Yes, he had told me how he felt... and he had definitely showed me. I felt the same connection that he did and it scared me. He had knocked on the door to my dark side, but was I ready to answer? I opened my eyes and tossed the card in the cup holder. Before I made my way to him, there was something I needed to do. I dropped the car into drive and pulled out of the garage, headed across town

***

No matter how many times I came here, I never got used to the sight of the elderly roaming the halls. Half not knowing where they were, while the rest hoped for some kind of affection. The strong medicinal smell always irritated my nose, and I swore I saw the shadow of death peeking around every corner. I approached the front desk and signed my name on the login sheet. After a short walk down the East hallway, I arrived at room fourteen. I entered and placed my purse down in the small chair by the window. She was asleep, so I gently sat on the bed next to her and took her fragile hand in my mine.

"Hi Mom," I whispered, "it's Violet." I watched as she slightly stirred. She had been through so much and had been in a nursing home for almost eight years. A ruptured aneurysm in her brain had almost claimed her life. Surgery saved her. But it cost her the ability to walk, plus she had a slight slur to her speech, and she was blind. After going through what I went through, I moved here to Chicago to be near her. She was my rock, and I knew I could come to her with anything.

I watched her sleep. The sun's rays bathed her room and her sleeping form in a golden glow. She looked so peaceful, so angelic. I didn't want to wake her, so I lightly stroked her hand one last time and got up from the bed. I walked back over to the chair to grab my purse and was turning to leave when I heard something.

"Violet, is that you?" Her voice was weak.

I walked back over to the bed and sat down. "Yes, mom it's me."

"My baby!" A smile lit up her tired face. "I'm so glad you came to see me."

I leaned up and kissed her on the forehead. "How are you feeling?"

She coughed, then cleared her throat. "I'm doing ok." She reached for my hand and patted it, then moved up my arm to my face. "Sweetie, is everything alright?"

Mom always had a way of knowing when something was going on with me. My silence gave me away. I sniffed and my tears started falling. I knew mom could feel the wetness on her hand.

"My dear girl, you're crying. What is troubling your heart?"

I couldn't hold it in any longer. "Oh mom, I'm so confused."

"Confused about what? Is it work?"

I couldn't bring myself to tell her I had gotten suspended. "No mom, work is ok."

"Are you feeling ok dear?"

"Yes mom, I feel fine."

She slid her hand down my face, back to my leg, and gently patted it. "It's a man, isn't it?"

My response was barely audible. "Yes."

"I see. What's the problem, sweetie?"

I got up from the bed and moved over in front of the window, staring out across the lush flowering gardens. "Well, it's not really a problem, I guess. It's just that I've met someone and we're very attracted to each other. We both feel a deep connection between us," I said, then hesitated. "But he is a famous musician."

Joy seeped into mom's voice. "That is so wonderful, honey! Famous, huh? Does that make a difference? If you both feel this way, then why are you confused?"

I walked back over and sat down on the edge of the bed. "Honestly, I don't know. Yes, he's famous, but I don't care about that. I want to know the man behind the persona. He has asked me to spend time with him before he goes back to Seattle. I don't know what to do. I'm afraid of opening myself up to him."

If mom only knew just *how* I had opened myself up to him…

"But now, he makes me want to share things with him. He makes me want to feel and experience life again, and I have tried so hard not to feel anything since…"

"Violet, now you listen to me, what happened to you was not your fault."

My tears rained down heavier as I leaned over and placed my head on her chest. The beating of her heart soothed me. "But I provoked it…"

"No, you didn't. No*body* deserves what happened to you. There is a place in hell for people like that. Now I may not have approved of the decisions you've made, but you did what you felt you had to do. But all those things are in the past now. You're my daughter and I love you. Everyone deserves a second chance, even you." She patted my head, smoothing her small, wrinkled fingers through my hair. "But I know you Violet, you always follow your head. This time, sweetie, you need to follow your heart."

I lifted off of mom's chest and reached for a Kleenex on the table by her bed, wiping my eyes and nose. "I love you too, mom and thank you for listening and understanding."

"Ms. Deveraux, it's time for your lunch," a nurse announced as she knocked on the door.

"Thank you Catherine. I will be ready in a moment."

"Ok, I'll be back shortly."

The nurse left, and I got up from the bed. "I'm going now, mom. I'll come see you again soon." While I fluffed her pillows, I helped her sit up and placed a kiss on her cheek. "I love you."

"I love you too, dear. Promise me you'll listen to what I said."

I teared up again as I patted her arm. "I will." After grabbing my purse, I headed back to the front desk to sign out.

***

I arrived home forty-five minutes later. Mom was right. My past was in the past and it was time to move on and enjoy life. And there was only one person I wanted to do that with. Before I went to see him, I went to the house to freshen up. I changed my clothes and hoped that what I wore would be to his liking. I spied the black box again. Now that Grayson knew what I used to be, I wondered if he would ever let me use the contents of the box on him. Even though he seemed to be the one who liked to dominate. My heart skipped a beat as I thought of the games we could play, if he was willing. The butterflies in my stomach grew as I climbed in the car and started toward the hotel. I couldn't wait to see my dark lover again.

CHAPTER THIRTEEN

My four black Goodyears rolled up in front of the hotel, and a young valet greeted me. I stepped out of the car and handed him the keys and a tip. As I stood on the sidewalk, I craned my neck up, admiring the size of the building. It was huge and very expensive-looking. The doorman opened the main door for me and I entered the lobby, headed for the front desk. I couldn't stop looking at the walls, the floors, the fountains, and the people. They all dripped with money.

"Good afternoon Miss," the dark-haired man in the freshly pressed suit and tie greeted. "How may I help you today?"

I reached into my purse and retrieved the card Grayson had given me. "Yes, I'm here to meet a friend. They are staying on the twelfth floor in the Infinity Suite. Can you tell me which way I should go?"

The desk clerk eyed me with an unbelieving look. "I see. Can you please tell me the guest's name?"

"Grayson Maddox," I reluctantly replied. I got the feeling that something wasn't right. "Is there a problem?"

He shifted his look away from me to his computer and started typing. A few moments later, he looked back up at me.

"I will need to make a phone call."

I now felt like Julia Roberts in Pretty Woman. I watched as he picked up his desk phone and punched a few buttons. A minute later, he hung up and turned back to me.

"Mr. Maddox is expecting you. Please take the elevator on your right to the twelfth floor. When you arrive, turn left."

"Thank you." I walked toward the golden glass elevators, pushed the up arrow on the right side, and climbed in. After pushing the number twelve button, the elevator began its climb. A few moments later, my black heels were sinking into red velour carpeting as I left the elevator and made my way down the left corridor. It surprised me to see that there weren't any security guards around. After a few more steps, I arrived at a huge white door. I raised my hand and gently tapped against it. This was it. There was no turning back. I didn't know what to expect, but I was ready for the possibilities.

The door opened and there he stood. No shirt, black sweatpants and barefoot. And his wavy amber locks hung in a loose ponytail. Our eyes locked as he spoke.

"You came."

I reached for his chest and ran my hands across it, twirling the coarse black hairs around my fingers. "I did a while ago... thanks to you."

A mischievous grin spread across his face as he stepped out of the doorway, allowing me to enter. "Come in, make yourself comfortable. Can I take your coat?"

"Uh no, that's alright." I said as I entered the suite and my eyes absorbed the enormity and the beauty of the space. The overhead chandelier, the plush furniture, and the gold piano in the corner were all amazing. But what really took my breath away was the surrounding view of the city that lay right outside the large windows. I walked over to one and peered out.

Grayson came up behind me and wrapped his arms around my waist. "Nice isn't it? It should be at six thousand dollars a night."

"Six thousand dollars? Wow."

My body stiffened. I suddenly felt out of my league. I would never in my life be able to afford anything like this. And yet here I was with a man who could. I dropped my gaze to the floor. Grayson loosened his hold and turned me around to face him, his finger lifting my chin to meet his hazel eyes.

"Hey, what's the matter?"

I flashed him a hint of a smile. "It's just that I've never been anywhere this nice before."

"But you are now." He leaned in and pecked my lips. "And you deserve to be here, understand?"

I nodded my head in agreement.

"Good. Now, what I really wanna know is why you came here," he reached for the front of my trench coat and wrapped his fingers around the loosely tied belt, "wearing nothing under your coat." He pulled it.

The coat fell open and my body shivered as the cool room air danced across my exposed flesh. I watched as Grayson's hands slid under the lapel and upward toward the collar. He pushed the black fabric across and over my shoulders, down my arms, where it fell to the floor in a pool around my feet.

"Did you do this for me?" his low tone questioned.

I nodded again.

His lean frame slowly circled around me, inspecting me. "What did you think would happen when you came here?"

My head dropped again toward the floor. "I... I thought that you..."

"You thought what, Violet? That I would fuck you?"

I stood silently

"I can't hear you. Answer me!"

His demanding voice sent a shock-wave through my body. "I don't know what I thought."

Grayson took a step back and reached for his face, stroking his beard.

"What if that coat had come open before you got here? Did you think about that?"

"No."

The swiftness of his body moving behind mine caught me off guard.

"Damn right you didn't. What if another man had seen what belonged to me?" he growled as he pushed me up against the window.

My breasts smashed against the coolness of the glass, bringing my nipples to stiff peaks. They were rubbing so hard against it, I was sure I was carving a mosaic masterpiece.

"Is that what you want? Every man in Chicago watching you, lusting after your body. Does that turn you on, Violet?"

A sudden gush of wetness coated my core and started running down my thighs. I was drowning in his words and burning from his touch.

Grayson rubbed his hand on my ass, then reached between my legs. "You've been bad, Violet," he said, bringing his wet fingers to my face, passing them under my nose, then across my lips. "And you know what happens to bad girls…" A dark laugh escaped him.

I swallowed hard and looked up at him, the fire in his hazel eyes consuming me.

"What are you going to do to me?"

He brought his fingers to his mouth and licked them one by one. "Anything I want."

My feet suddenly left the ground as Grayson scooped me up and carried me toward the bedroom. A few steps later, I was being deposited onto a king sized bed covered with black silk sheets. The heavy gold and black drapes blocked out the sun, and the only light being produced was coming from the lamp sitting on each nightstand.

"Get on all fours and don't move!" he commanded. "And leave your heels on."

I did as I was told, lowering the top half of my body down onto my arms and elbows while sticking my ass up in the air. I then felt the bed dip as Grayson climbed in behind me.

"My sweet Violet, we're gonna play a game."

Oh shit, I knew I was in for it now. "What kind of game?" I nervously asked, turning my head to look behind me.

"Eyes forward!" he growled.

I turned back around and faced the headboard.

"It's going to be a guessing game. And to make sure you don't peek, I have something for you."

The bed creaked as he rose and climbed over my body. My vision suddenly darkened as he covered my eyes with a blindfold.

"Now, before we begin, I have some ground rules that you are going to follow."

My body trembled with both fear and excitement.

"Rule number one, when you and I are together outside of the bedroom, you will refer to me as Mr. Maddox."

He rubbed his hand across the dip of my back and down to my ass, slowly caressing each cheek.

"Rule number two, when we are inside of the bedroom, you will call me Sir or Daddy. From now on you will be my Pet."

He placed a light kiss against the fleshy folds of my pussy.

"And rule number three, you will no longer call that son of a bitch Biff Cartwell — sir. You're my girl... not his!"

He snuck a finger inside my core.

"I'm gonna test your limits baby, I just hope you know them. If we have to use a safe word, we will. Each time you disobey a rule, you'll be punished as I see fit. Do you understand everything I have just said?"

I was quiet for a moment before I answered him. "Yes."

Grayson's tone lowered and danger flavored his words. "Good. Now let's begin..."

The bed lifted, and I heard him climb off and walk around the room. A few seconds later, the thumping of dance music filled the room. I heard a drawer open and shut, then felt Grayson climb back on the bed. There was stillness for a moment, before I felt something hard sneak between my fleshy folds and press firmly against my clit.

"Tell me my Pet, what that is this?"

I blurted out the first thing that came to my mind. "It feels like a dick."

The aging rocker roared with a dark laugh. "Wrong answer!"

A loud smack landed on my ass, and I jumped.

"Ow!"

"Try again!"

This time, the object rubbed against my clit, then plunged into my core, creeping in and out. I didn't know what it was, but the sensation it was causing felt exquisite.

"Grayson, I don't know what —"

SMACK

"What did you call me?"

I swiftly corrected myself. "I'm sorry Sir... I didn't mean to call you... I don't know what it is."

The object inside of me started buzzing.

"Do you know now?"

My body came to life with the sensation between my legs. "Ohhh... yes... it's a... vibrator."

"Good job, Pet!" Grayson praised as he guided the unit in and out of me, circling it against my clit. My eyes rolled back in my head and my breathing quickened. He must have noticed that I was enjoying it just a little too much.

"That's enough!" He pulled the vibrator away. "Wouldn't want you to come already... let's see if you can guess the next one."

My heart beat wildly with anticipation as I felt Grayson return to my pussy and shove the next item into it.

"Fuck!" I shrieked at the hard coldness that violated me. "It's an ice cube!"

He reprimanded me with another hard smack. "Wrong!"

My moist heat gradually adjusted to the smooth, cold object as it worked its way in and out of my core. "Is it another vibrator?"

"NO!"

SMACK

"You know, Pet, red is suddenly becoming my new favorite color."

I exhaled a sharp breath, reeling from the slap. "Why is that Sir?"

"Because your ass and your pussy are both a lovely shade of it. Now come on, I'm waiting for an answer!"

He continued his torture with the cold object as my arms and legs tired. My body slumped. "I don't know Sir."

"Are you tiring on my already Pet? We haven't even started." He reached around my waist and jerked my body back up into position. "Alright, I'll give you that one. It was a frozen glass dildo."

Damn. Not a dildo, but a frozen dildo. I wondered what he would inflict on me next.

"Well, Pet, although I'm *not* pleased with your first lesson, I'm going to have mercy on you. What do you say?"

I turned my head toward him. "Thank you, Sir."

"That's right. And now I think it's time for a little reward. Don't move!"

My body, although exhausted, tingled with anticipation at what my reward would be. He left the bed and soon returned. This time, he was standing by the headboard. I felt his hands lightly brush against my face and remove the blindfold.

"This time I want you to watch."

He bent down and softly kissed my lips. "Do you trust me?"

The words came easily. "Yes daddy, I do."

"So beautiful," he cooed, skimming his hand along the curve of my body before moving behind me. The sound of his descending zipper echoed over the music and crashed against my ears.

As soon as the warm slick substance fell onto my skin, I knew what it was and I knew what was going to happen. Grayson smoothed his large hand through the lube and caressed my full ass. Easing my cheeks apart, he lazily rubbed a coated finger around the outside of my little puckered hole, taking a test dip. My whole body tensed at the invasion. It had been a long time since I had done this.

"Relax," he soothed.

I took a deep breath and relaxed my body as he tested the waters again, this time dipping his finger in and out in a rhythmic motion.

"Uhhh..." It felt so good.

"Turn around Pet. I want you to watch."

I turned my head to look over my shoulder and watched as Grayson cradled his cock in his hand He coated it with a generous amount of lube, smearing it along the veiny shaft and around the bulbous head. My arousal heightened at the sight, and wetness dripped out of me. It hardened at his touch and my eyes widened at the size and girth of it. I guessed he had to be at least 7 inches. He must have sensed my trepidation.

"Don't worry, it'll fit as long as I take it slow," he smirked. "Are you ready?"

My eyes stayed connected with his hazel ones as I licked my lips. "Yes, daddy... make me yours."

I turned my head back around and prepared myself for what was about to happen. My dark lover once again parted my ass, slowly rubbed the head of his slathered cock against my hole, then gently pushed the tip in.

"Ooh...Uhhh..."

I bunched the sheets in my hand and willed my body to relax as he continued to bury the head of his cock inside of me.

"Fuck... baby... you're so tight!"

He stopped for a moment to allow me to adjust to his size. At first it was uncomfortable, but the little waves of pleasure that began coursing through my core made me hungry for more.

"Keep going," I panted. "Give it all to me."

"Are you sure?" he hesitantly questioned.

"Yes! I want you to —"

"You want me to what? I want to hear you say it. Tell daddy what you want!"

With everything inside of me, I unleashed a scream from the depths of my soul. I was sure the entire hotel heard me. "I want you to fuck my ass!"

And with that, Grayson Maddox rammed his entire cock inside of me. Over and over he plunged all the way in, then pulled all the way out, keeping in time with the heavy bass. My whole body was on fire. The silk sheets scraped against my nipples as my breasts swung back and forth from the force. He grabbed a handful of my hair and yanked it as he rode me.

"Ah fuck! Baby, you're so good!"

I snuck my hand down to play with my clit as I lifted my ass higher and pushed back against his every thrust. My blood was boiling, and I was seeing stars.

"Keep... going... almost... there."

I felt the fire ignite in my loins and spread across my body. I was going to come... and come hard.

"I'm gonna come too, baby. Uhhh..."

Grayson unleashed a few more solid thrusts as my orgasm claimed me. "AHHHHH!"

He quickly pulled out and spurt his warm spunk all over my ass and lower back. "FUUUUCK!"

I collapsed on the bed and Grayson bent over me, bracing himself with his hands on either side of me, both of us fighting to regain our breath and composure. I turned on my side to face him. He smoothed a finger across my back, then brought it to my lips. I instinctively opened my mouth and swallowed his seed.

"That... was..."

He smiled at me. "Incredible."

I ran my hand down his face, and he kissed my thumb.

"Rest now Pet."

I smiled at him as he climbed across the bed to join me on the other side, pulling me into his powerful arms. Soon, we both drifted into a sweet slumber.

CHAPTER FOURTEEN

Sometime later I stirred to life, awakening from the most wonderful dream involving Grayson. I shifted in the bed and a sharp pain radiated from my backside around to my pelvis. My eyes shot open at the realization that it wasn't a dream. Our actions from only a few hours ago played on the screen in my mind. It was so real... so raw. I couldn't believe that I had allowed him to take control of me so easily. I was not the type to let men dominate me. And yet, with him, it was different. I rolled over to reach for my dark lover and found nothing but an empty space. The cool silk sheets sliding through my fingers told me he had left the bed some time ago. I rolled back over, climbed out of the bed and stretched. It was time to indulge in a nice, long shower.

As steam filled the room, I slid the glass shower door open and stepped in, jolting as I stepped under the hot spray. I let the water flow through my hair, cascade over my skin, and soothe my sore muscles. I reached for the bottle of body wash sitting on the small shelf in the corner and opened it. The smell of vanilla, caramel, and macadamia greeted my senses. It smelled like him. I squeezed the bottle, letting the soap drizzle all over my body. As I circled my breasts, a shot of arousal coursed through me. I closed my eyes and started imaging Grayson standing there with me.

My hands continued lower, across my stomach, and down to my dark patch of curls. I dipped a finger inside and moaned. Quickly adding another finger, I began a rhythmic motion. My head fell back against the shower wall and my eyes slammed shut. I was so lost in my fantasy that I never heard the person who entered the bathroom and was now stepping into the shower with me. My fingers were jerked away from my center and replaced by another pair. I opened my eyes and came face to face with my angel. He continued to work his magic on me as we stared into each others eyes.

"Don't think... just feel," his deep voice soothed.

He moved closer and started kissing my lips, moving along my jawline and down my neck, sucking and nibbling against my pulse. I was ready to come. He bent his head down to my breasts, sucking the left one into his moist mouth, his teeth grazing my nipple, before reciprocating the feeling on the right one. I raised my leg and placed my foot on the corner shelf, allowing him deeper access as he continued to work my body. My body tensed as my orgasm built and I shuttered. I couldn't hold on anymore.

"Let it go baby..." he whispered.

A parade of colors danced in my vision as my walls spasmed and I succumbed to his touch. He withdrew his fingers and brought them to my lips, guiding them into my mouth. I ran my tongue around them, coating it with my tangy essence. Grayson removed his fingers and brought them to his own lips. As he did this, I realized this was the first time I had actually seen his manhood up close. My eyes wandered along the thick length, then back up across his solid frame, returning to his gaze. He noticed what I was doing and smirked.

"Tell me, Violet, do you like what you see?"

My entire body blushed.

He reached for my hand and guided it to his cock. "Touch me baby... explore my body."

I couldn't believe how shy I had suddenly become. For crying out loud, that monster was inside of me just a few hours ago.

I smoothed my fingers across his narrow hips, then wrapped them around the base. He shuddered beneath my hand as I glided it along his meaty length all the way to the tip, lazily rubbing my thumb around the head, then back down again. He turned and moved back against the shower wall, leaning his head against it as he closed his eyes. I quickened my pace and a soft moan crossed his lips. My arousal grew again as I watched the effect I had on him. I was now dominating him. Women around the world would've killed to be in my position right now. I let go of his dick and he opened his eyes, giving me a questioning look.

A devilish grin spread across my face as I dropped to my knees before him. I tilted my head up to meet his hazel gaze as he intertwined his fingers in my hair. His sexy voice enticed me.

"Taste me..."

I skimmed my fingertips lightly around the base of his cock, circling around and under his scrotum, before leaning forward and guiding him into my moist mouth. His full size hit the back of my throat and I choked. I took a deep breath, relaxed my gag reflex, and swallowed him whole, causing him to cry out.

"Oh, shit!"

I wrapped my hands around him and twisted them in opposite directions as I bobbed up and down, running my tongue along his length, swirling it around the head. Lapping up the pearly drops of pre-come that appeared. His grasp on my hair tightened, and I looked up at him. His eyes were now shut, and he was panting. I moved one of my hands to reach for his thinly skinned sack, lightly skimming it with my fingernail. I sucked him a few more times before moving my lips to kiss down his shaft and under it to his balls. Opening my mouth, I sucked one of them in, licking and nibbling on the fragile globe before showering the other one with the same attention. Grayson's body tensed, and I knew he was teetering on the edge of no return.

I returned my mouth to envelop him once more, and he wasted no time grabbing my head.

"Look at me!" he commanded, his baritone echoing off the shower walls.

I looked up at him and our eyes locked as he began fucking my face with a vengeance.

"Damn babygirl you're so good…"

I reached up and braced my hands against his legs for support as he picked up speed and raced toward the finish line.

"Get ready… uhhhh… cause this bad boy… ooohh… is coming… ahhh fuuuckkkk!"

The warm salty substance flowed in copious amounts from his cock, onto the velvet of my tongue and down my throat. After one final snap of his hips, he let go of my head and I pulled him from my mouth. I gave him a sexy look as I swallowed the last drop. He offered his hand and helped me up from the shower floor, wrapping his arms around my waist, pulling me close.

"Thank you," he said, giving me a passionate kiss.

I smiled at him seductively. "Anytime… daddy."

He smacked my ass, and I jumped. "I think we really need to clean up now. I have a surprise for you."

I looked at him seriously. I knew what my surprise was last time and was not ready for a repeat anytime soon.

"No, it's not that," he chuckled. "I know you're sore. Finish your shower and you'll see."

He gave me one last peck on the lips and I watched him climbed out of the shower. That man had one of the finest asses I had ever seen. I hurried up and washed off under the now cold water, then turned it off. I grabbed one of the white plush towels from the rack along the wall and wrapped it around my body before stepping out and heading back to the bedroom.

CHAPTER FIFTEEN

When I entered the room, I immediately drew my eyes to a large white box with a blue bow wrapped around it sitting at the foot of the bed. I walked over and slid the satin bow off the lid and carefully opened the box.

"Oh my God!" The contents made me squeal in sheer delight. It was a beautiful lavender silk dress trimmed in delicate black lace. I held it against the front of my body and instantly knew it would fit perfectly. I gently laid it on the bed and returned to the box. Next, I found a sexy black strapless bra with matching lace thong panties. I smoothed my fingers across them before placing them alongside the dress. And last, in the box's bottom were two items wrapped in tissue paper. I carefully removed the paper and found a pair of matching purple heels. They were exquisite, and I instantly fell in love with the black rose adorning each side. I excitedly sat down and tried one on. It fit perfectly. I felt like Cinderella trying on the glass slipper. How in the hell did Grayson know my size? I took the shoe off and stood back up as he walked into the room.

"I hope you like them," he chimed, propped up against the doorway like a Playgirl pin-up. He was wearing a suit in the same lavender color with matching black boots. His hair was down and still damp. The water made it look darker, and it contrasted to the stands of gray that peeked through. How did he get dressed so fast?

"I love them! And the dress is beautiful, thank you," I beamed. "But why did you buy them? They must've cost a fortune."

He sauntered over to me and snaked his arms around my waist. "Because one, you have no clothes, remember? And two, the restaurant won't let you in naked."

I let out a light laugh. "Yes, I remember. Well, that was very nice of you to do that for me. Are we going to dinner?"

"You're welcome. And yes, they have a wonderful restaurant downstairs and after what happened today," he leaned in and kissed me, "I've worked up quite an appetite."

I kissed him back. "Me too."

"Go ahead and finish getting ready. I have an extra bag of makeup in the cabinet you can use. I'll be in the living room."

It sounded funny to hear him say he had a bag of makeup. But that was his style. It was part of who he was, and I accepted that. I just hoped that one day he would be comfortable enough to feel like he didn't need to wear it around me.

I finished drying off, then slipped on my bra and panties. I then reached for the dress, stepped into it and worked it up my body. It fit like a glove. I scrunched the towel through my hair twice before heading to the bathroom to use the blow-dryer. A few minutes later, I reached into the cabinet for the makeup bag and put some on. I returned to the bedroom, slid on my heels, then headed for the living room. He was tinkering with the keys on the gold piano. I snuck up behind him and wrapped my arms around his neck, placing a kiss on his temple.

"What were you playing? It sounded nice."

He turned and lightly kissed my forearm. "Just something that's been rolling around in my head. Maybe I'll let you hear it another time. Are you ready?"

I released my hold. "Yep."

Grayson stood as I grabbed my purse from the coffee table, and soon we headed out the door.

After taking the elevator down to the second floor, we entered the dining area where the Maître D' welcomed us.

"Ah, good evening Mr. Maddox, right this way, sir."

We followed behind the tall French man in the tuxedo to our table, where he gracefully pulled the chair out for me and I sat down. Grayson then took his seat. There were some gawkers staring at us as we walked by their tables. It was just something that I had to get used to if I was going to be seen with a famous musician.

"Your waiter this evening will be Jacques. Thank you for being our guests."

My eyes scanned the room as the Maître D' left. "This place is amazing!"

Grayson smiled. "Yeah it is. I enjoy coming here when I'm in Chicago. I know the chef personally. I met him when we were on tour in France."

"That's so cool."

Our waiter arrived and introduced himself as he handed each of us a menu. Grayson told him to give us a few minutes, and he scurried away. I opened my menu and immediately noticed there were no prices. I glanced up and saw a familiar pair of hazel eyes staring over-top of their menu at me.

"What's wrong?"

I looked up at him. "Umm, I've never seen a menu without prices."

A genuine laugh escaped him. "This ain't McDonald's baby. Don't worry about the price, just get whatever you want. I've got it."

For some reason, his comment hit me the wrong way. I closed my menu and laid it on the table. "Look, I appreciate everything you have done for me, the clothes and shoes, now dinner. Other women may have expected these things from you. But I don't want you to think that I'm that type of woman. I've always paid my own way."

Grayson raised his voice as anger flowed from him. "And what exactly makes you think that I'm not just trying to be nice? Huh? What's wrong with sharing things with someone you care about?"

Jacques returned to take our orders, starting with me. I ordered shrimp linguini with white wine sauce while Grayson ordered spring pasta with fried eggplant, along with a bottle of red wine. Jacques nodded his approval, then disappeared back into the kitchen, leaving Grayson and I looking at each other in awkward silence.

"I'm sorry. I didn't mean to sound bitchy." My hand reached across the table for his. "You just have to be patient with me. It's been a long time since someone has treated me right. I do appreciate everything you've done for me."

Grayson continued staring at me, his face void of any emotion, his eyes burning a hole through me. He jerked his hand out of mine and, after what seemed like an eternity, he finally found his voice.

"So tell me, Violet, how did you become a dominatrix?"

CHAPTER SIXTEEN

And there it was. The inevitable question. Hanging in the air like an early morning California smog. It wouldn't have mattered if he asked it now or ten years from now. I would never be prepared to answer it. I could never tell him my whole story. I wanted to run far away and never look back. But my heart wouldn't let me. As I continued to look at him, the emotionless stare masking his eyes told me he was serious. He deserved honesty. I just hoped that he would understand what I was about to tell him. I reached for my water glass and took a long drink before I began.

"Well, I think it's best to start at the beginning. I grew up here in Illinois and had a normal childhood. I was a little girl in love with Barbie, stickers and unicorns. Life was good and although my parents would fight now and then, I had no doubt that they loved me. But as I got older, I noticed they were becoming distant. My dad was drinking more and their fighting became intense."

"I can relate to the fighting parents," Grayson quietly chimed in, his warm almond eyes glancing down briefly, then back up. "Sorry, go ahead."

"One night, right after my seventeenth birthday, I realized the depth of darkness that had been consuming my father. He came home drunk and my mom confronted him about having an affair, to which he admitted. She went ballistic and came at him with a butcher knife. He flew into a rage and slammed her against the refrigerator. The knife fell out of her hand and dad threw her on the floor. He sat on top of her, grabbed the knife, and started stabbing her. After he stopped, he repeatedly punched her in the head until she was unconscious. I had been standing in the hallway watching the whole time and started screaming and crying. Dad snapped his head in my direction, jumped off of mom and started chasing after me, the knife still in his hand."

The memory of that night was so vivid in my mind. My heart broke all over again as I envisioned my mother lying on the kitchen floor defenseless and almost lifeless. The demonic glare in my father's eyes shook me to my core.

Grayson shook his head in disbelief. "Holy shit! Then what happened?"

"He chased me through the living room, then back to my bedroom. He grabbed me and backhanded me, knocking me across the bed. I climbed back up and moved against the headboard, trying to block him with my hands and a pillow, but he kept waving the blade at me, the sharp metal slicing the tender flesh of my hands and arms. I was hysterical and screamed at him to stop, but he wouldn't. The only thing that saved me was the ringing of our doorbell. He paused long enough to drop the knife and ran out of the room. I heard some voices followed by a door slam, and a few minutes later, our neighbor Lori was comforting me."

Grayson's stoic face softened and there was something in his eyes I had never seen before — sorrow.

"Violence is bad enough, but when it happens to you at the hands of someone you love and trust..." The hurt tone of his voice resonated with me so much. It was as if he could relate to what I was saying. "Were you ok? What happened to your mom?"

"Well, after Lori found me, I led her to the kitchen, and we found mom laying there. Her face was unrecognizable and there was blood everywhere. I kneeled beside her and covered what wounds I could with my hands, holding pressure on them to stop the bleeding while Lori called 911. A few minutes later, an ambulance arrived, and the police were coming through the door. She told the police that she heard screams and came over to see if everything was ok. After she rang the doorbell, my father jerked the door open and ran out of the house screaming, 'I think I killed her'. Two EMTs loaded mom onto a gurney and rushed her to the hospital, while the rest of them stayed and treated my cuts and bruises. I then gave my statement to the police."

Grayson rested his elbows on the table and folded his hands on top of each other, resting his chin. "Did they ever catch your crazy son of a bitch father?"

My eyes darted to the table while my fingers skimmed across the white linen covering it. "Actually, they found his body about two hours later. He had jumped off the bridge near our house and landed on the bed of boulders below. I had not only lost my father, but I didn't know if my mom would survive." My shaky hand reached for another sip of water. "But by some miracle, she did. The stab wounds had missed her major organs. They released her from the hospital almost a month later. My aunt and uncle claimed my father's body and held his funeral. I didn't go. As much as I loved my father, I just couldn't forgive him. I still haven't."

My dark lover reached across the table and gathered my hands into the worn gentleness of his own. "I'm so sorry, baby, that you had to go through all that. How did you and your mom survive?"

My eyes met his sincere ones. "Well, mom wasn't the same after everything that happened and she sank into a deep depression and couldn't work."

Jacques returned to our table with our food and opened our bottle of Cabernet Sauvignon. "I hope everything is satisfactory. Please enjoy!" Grayson and I both thanked him and I continued.

"We used what money mom and dad had saved, but when it ran out, I dropped out of school and went to work as a waitress at a restaurant in town."

Grayson took a bite of his pasta. "What happened to your family? That's not fair that you had to quit school and take on so much responsibility at seventeen. But then again, who am I to talk?"

I briefly pondered the last part of his statement as I poured a glass of wine and brought it to my lips. "They wanted nothing to do with us and blamed my mom for pushing dad to drink and have the affair."

"Man, that's some bullshit! How long did you work at the diner?"

I relished in my first bite of shrimp. "Well, for the first two years I made money, paid the bills and took care of mom. Then everything changed the third year I was there. A guy named Matt started coming in and eventually became a regular. He was smart, funny, and we shared banter all the time. He would always say, "why is a pretty girl like you working in a dive like this?""

The middle-aged rocker scrunched his face at the mention of Matt's name. "Sounds like he had the hots for you. Did you go out with him?"

"No, it was nothing like that. But what happened is one day he offered me a business opportunity."

"And what was that?" Grayson savored another bite of his eggplant.

I hesitated and swallowed hard. The answer crossed my lips in a quiet tone.

"He asked me to star in a porn film."

Grayson's eyes became the size of saucers and his body tensed as he laid down his fork and reached for the wine. He filled his glass to the brim and drank almost all of it in one gulp. "Continue."

"I was very unsure and refused at first, but when he told me how much money I would make, all I could think about was how much it would help mom. So I agreed to it."

"Hmmm..." His eyes were glued to me. "Did you tell her what you were doing?"

I shook my head. "No. I couldn't. She thought I was working at the diner. And besides that, she had moved to Chicago to live with her sister. So eventually, I was on my own."

"So what happened to the movie?" He grabbed for his glass again.

"On the day we shot the film, Matt drove me to a large warehouse where I was briefly introduced to my co-star Larry Loins and the film crew. I didn't know what to do or how to act. Matt told me to relax and let Larry take the lead, just do what came naturally. But there was one minor detail I didn't share with them."

"What was that?"

"I was a virgin."

CHAPTER SEVENTEEN

Grayson damn near spit out the last of his wine. "You mean to tell me you lost your virginity to some sleazy guy in a porn movie? Shit! And here I thought screwing at twelve years old was bad."

Now I was curious. "You had sex at twelve?"

"Yeah, I did. But we're not talkin' about me mama, I wanna know what happened with you."

I shrugged my shoulders and took another bite of food. "There's nothing much to tell. Larry took the lead and popped my cherry in front of the entire world. And as the camera continued to roll, I overcame my shyness and got up enough gumption to take my first lesson in dick sucking."

Grayson Maddox was beyond agitated. He pushed his plate to the side, covering it with his cloth napkin, and blew out a long breath. "Did he use a condom or fuck you raw?"

"What?"

"Did you let him come inside you, or did he pull out?"

"He pulled out."

"Did you spit or swallow?"

"I spit. Why the hell does any of this matter?"

"Was that the only time you were with him?" His voice was thick with jealously and crimson anger colored his face.

I sighed. "No. I made two more movies with him."

He drew in his bottom lip and sucked his teeth. "I see. So let me get this right, before you were a dominatrix, you were a porn star."

I knew he was pissed. And that's why I didn't want to tell him. But if he couldn't handle this, how would he take what else I had to say?

"I don't look at myself as a porn star. I just did what I had to do to make money."

"But there were other ways of making money, Violet." He poured another glass of wine and it disappeared in seconds. "Was Larry the one that got you in the dominatrix business?"

"No, that was Matt too."

He cringed again at the sound of Matt's name.

"One night we went out to dinner, and he ended up taking me to an S&M club. At first, I was taken aback by what I was watching. But then I was asked to take part. My curiosity got the best of me, and so I did."

"Matt just has all the ideas, doesn't he?" Grayson huffed sarcastically. "Did you enjoy it?"

A small smile graced my lips. "Honestly, I did. The first time someone handed me a flogger, and I smacked someone's ass, it was like I became a different person. I felt empowered. Matt and I visited the club a few more times, and I started getting requests for one-on-one sessions. So he and I became business partners. He rented a small building which I used as my dungeon, and he would book the clients and collect the money."

The Rancid Orchid singer shifted in his chair and smoothed his hand across his coarse beard. "Dungeon, huh?" A hint of curiosity flashed in his eyes. "What kinda things did you do?"

"Most of my clients were businessmen, executives in high-ranking positions. They had to be in charge all the time and they wanted some kind of release from that. I also had others who were just curious. There was no intercourse involved, but they could perform oral sex on me if they paid extra. Each session really depended on what the client wanted. Some things I have been involved in and used include bondage, humiliation, nipple clamps, cock rings and anal plugs, vibrators, dildos, spanking, flogging and whipping, ball gags, electricity play and mummification."

I looked at Grayson. I could see the wheels turning in his mind, but I couldn't make out his expression. "Are you alright? I know this is a lot to take in."

He cleared his throat and pushed his chair back. "Umm... that's some serious shit, babygirl. And honestly, I don't know how I feel about all of it." His voice deepened. "Especially the thought of all those guys eatin' you out. And if they paid for it, isn't that considered prostitution?"

Why did he have to push my bitch button?

"Well, first of all, I'm not a prostitute. And as far as all those guys eatin' my pussy, I've said nothing to you about all the women who've sucked your dick or you've fucked!" I was pissed. "And second, you wanted to know about my past, so I told you! If you can't accept it, that's your problem, not mine!."

He was on the verge of exploding and got defensive. "Yeah, but women don't pay me to suck my dick or fuck me. They just line up wherever I go! That's the perks of being famous, baby. And you're right, I wanted to know about your past. Don't worry, cause I can take ANYTHING that is thrown at me." He leaned back and ran both hands through his long locks. "But there's still one thing I wanna know. How the hell did you go from fuckin' in porn films and beatin' asses to workin' for Biff Cartwell in Chicago? Somethin' just doesn't add up, sweetheart."

I didn't know why he couldn't leave well enough alone and accept what I told him. I twirled the last bite of linguini around my fork, dipped it in the last drops of sauce on my plate, and scarfed it down.

"Does it really matter? Let's not talk about this anymore." I flashed him a nervous smile. "Let's just try to have an enjoyable time."

But I knew Grayson and he wouldn't be satisfied until he had all the answers he wanted.

"Actually, it matters. I still want to know Violet, so why won't you tell me?"

I took a deep breath and silently prayed that I could get through the entire story without coming apart. It was now or never.

"Many men came and went through my door. But there was one who came through that was different. His name was Adam. He was a big, powerful guy, yet he had a vulnerability to him. It was a vulnerability that I drew on in his sessions, and that also made him attractive. He became a regular and as time went on, I developed feelings for him. But my cardinal rule was to never fall in love with a client. One day after his session, he admitted he was falling in love with me. And without thinking, I admitted I was falling for him, too. I'll never forget the look of sheer joy on his face. That was until I told him that even though I had feelings for him, I would never act on them. I told him our relationship had to remain strictly professional. He told me he understood and left. At the end of the day, I was preparing to leave and as I stepped out the door to head to my car..."

All the noise and people around me slowly drifted into the background as I lapsed into tunnel vision, burning a hole through the plate in front of me. I was unconsciously wringing my hands and my insides were shaking. I felt like I was going to vomit.

"What happened?"

I could hear Grayson's voice off in the distance.

"Violet? Are you ok?"

I heard him again and looked up. Those beautiful brown eyes were hanging on my every word. He needed to know, and I wanted to tell him... but I just couldn't find the words. I could feel the wetness pooling in the corners of my eyes and it would only take one blink to release the flood.

"I... I have to go."

I jumped out of my chair, grabbed my purse and took off through the dining room toward the elevators. I'm sure the restaurant patrons were enjoying the entertainment we were providing.

"Violet!" Grayson's voice rumbled behind me.

I reached the elevators and continuously pushed the down button, almost breaking my nail. The longer I waited for the door to open, the closer the sound of his voice came. The thumping of his boots against the marble floor told me he was near. I threw my head over my shoulder and looked dead into his face. So I took off toward the stairwell. Pushing the heavy door open, I ran down the narrow stairs as fast as my four-inch heels would let me. I came to a stop at the door that led into the main lobby and jerked it open. Dodging people and luggage carriers in a Hail Mary play, I sprinted on my way to the front door exit.

"VIOLET!"

Damn, he was still hot on my trail and he was catching up to me. I wanted to turn around again, but I didn't. I stormed past the doorman and out onto the curb, asking the valet to please hurry with my car. Pacing back and forth, I kept a wary eye on the door. A wave of relief washed over me when I saw my Firebird rolling up the driveway. The valet jumped out, and I started toward the driver's side.

I was going to make it.

Then something grabbed my arm and spun me around.

"What the hell is wrong with you?!"

I looked at the ground and prayed it would open up and swallow me whole.

Grayson's grip on my arms tightened as he shook me. "Violet, look at me, damn it! What the fuck happened?"

I couldn't take it anymore. I released the flood as I lifted my eyes to him and found my voice.

"THAT MOTHERFUCKER RAPED AND BEAT ME!"

Jerking loose from his hold, I stormed away. I got in the car, dropped it down into drive, and sped off. My body heaved with sobs as I glanced in the rearview mirror. He was still standing on the curb, looking dumbfounded.

I never wanted to hurt him.

But I had.

I never wanted him to know the whole truth.

But now he did.

And now, I didn't know what to do.

CHAPTER EIGHTEEN

I roared into my driveway and killed the engine. My head slumped against the steering wheel while my fingers maintained their death grip. I was crying so hard that I couldn't catch my breath. The crushing pain in my chest mixed with the emotional dagger piercing my heart was too much to bear. I slowly climbed out of the car and dragged myself into the house. Stumbling through the darkness and into the living room, I kicked off my heels and collapsed onto the couch, grabbing one of the small decorative pillows lying to the side, clutching it to my chest. Reliving the violation that happened to me clawed at my soul. And now that Grayson knew all of my dark secrets, I didn't know how he would ever accept someone like me. I cried until no more tears would come. Exhaustion set in and sleep was claiming me. As my eyes fluttered shut, I heard a noise at the door. I turned my head and my strained voice produced a squeak.

"Go away."

The jingling of the turning knob made me realize that during my emotional turmoil, I'd forgotten to lock the door.

"I said go the fuck away!"

The door opened, and a figure entered, heading toward me. I hugged the pillow tighter as I sat up and started shaking. It was like experiencing my nightmare all over again.

"I'm afraid I can't do that, Violet."

I knew that sexy baritone.

He reached for the lamp on the end table, and with a click, the room flooded with light. Sitting down on the couch, he turned to look at me and shook his head.

"You followed me?"

"Does it matter?" His long fingers reached for my leg and began skimming the soft flesh there, relaxing me. I sighed at his touch. It made me want to forget everything, but I knew I had to finish telling him what happened. I drew a shaky breath, looked up at his beautiful careworn face, and continued.

"I walked out the door and felt someone push me back in. The gentle face I knew was now full of hatred and rage. He grabbed my purse from my shoulder and threw it across the room, then slammed me to the floor. He climbed on top of me, pinning me with his large legs, and ripped off my shirt and bra before jerking down my pants. All he kept saying was that he loved me and that I belonged to him. I started screaming, and he punched me. As he raped me, he continued to beat me. I begged and pleaded with him to stop, but he didn't. He rammed inside of me and after a few excruciating thrusts, he came, then climbed off. Blood poured from my face and head as I rolled over, pooling on the floor. I was crying hysterically."

I studied Grayson's face for any kind of reaction. There wasn't any. The soft light coming from the lamp highlighted the wrinkles and crow's feet that were produced from the wild life he had lived. I focused on them as I continued with my story.

"As he zipped up his pants, he walked back over and told me to shut up. I then felt a sharp pain radiated through my body as he kicked me in the ribs. He looked down at me and called me a whore before spitting on me. His maniacal laugh echoed throughout the room as he left, slamming the door behind him. My last conscious thoughts were of my mom. She had gone through a lot at the hands of my father. And now I understood her pain. I thought about how disappointed she was going to be with me. I felt the warm stickiness of the blood as it trickled into my eyes, matting them shut. My world then became a black void. A beeping noise was the first thing I remembered when I came to. I opened my eyes and saw that I was in a hospital. The beeping was my heart monitor."

The rubbing on my leg stopped. "Who found you?"

"Matt did. He said that when he went to leave, he saw my car was still in the parking lot. He called for me and when I didn't answer, he went looking for me and found me on the floor. I was in the hospital for a week with a concussion, a broken nose, and bruised ribs. The only thing I can be thankful for is that I didn't get pregnant."

Grayson rose and slid over closer, wrapping his arm around my shoulder, stroking it. "Please tell me that motherfucker is in jail."

I started sniffling again. "He is. Matt gave the police his information, and they arrested him. He confessed to everything, and they charged him with first degree rape and aggravated assault and battery. Once they locked him away, and I knew I was safe, I called my aunt in Chicago and asked if I could come and stay with her and mom. I found out that not long after mom moved there, she suffered a ruptured aneurysm and almost died. I hurried up and packed my car and drove to Chicago to be with her... and to start my life over."

"Why didn't your aunt call you and tell you about your mom? That's some bullshit. How is she now?"

"She's in a nursing home near here. The aneurysm left her blind. Her speech is slurred and she can't walk. But she is in good spirits. The hardest thing I ever had to do was tell her what I had been doing and what happened to me. It broke her heart."

My dark lover's hand trailed up the back of my neck and his fingers smoothed through my hair, tenderly massaging my scalp. "Wow. But at least you are here and can see her now."

"Yes, and I am thankful to still have her. And to answer your question, once I got here and got settled, I bounced from job to job until Biff took a chance and hired me. I knew nothing about being an Administrative Assistant but I learned how to bluff my way through."

Grayson rolled his eyes and scoffed. "Yeah, good ol' Biff. He should kiss the ground you walk on for putting up with his sorry ass for this long!"

I forced a small smile.

He smiled back as he turned his purple suited body to face me, wrapping his other arm around my body. The musky scent of his cologne intoxicated my senses as I drowned in the depths of his hazel orbs. Time seemed to stand still as our lips gravitated toward each other like two magnets. The kiss was gentle, but we could both feel the underlying want and need. He increased the pressure, and the couch dipped as he lowered his body onto mine. The ache in my heart and the void in my soul were what I wanted him to ease. I needed him to take away my feelings of unworthiness and make me feel whole again. I reached for his hair and threaded my fingers through it. Breaking the kiss, I whispered in his ear.

"Make love to me."

He dropped his head to the sweet spot on my neck and sucked.

I pleaded. "Grayson... please make love to me."

He stopped and pulled away, sitting up on the couch. "As much as I want to do that, I don't think it's the best thing right now."

I twisted my face in disbelief. "You're kidding me, right?"

"No." He let out a long, heavy breath. "You're not in the right frame of mind, and I don't want us to do something that we both would regret."

My sadness quickly became anger. "Regret? How could making love be a regret considering all the other things we've done? I thought you cared about me? Cause I sure as hell care about you!"

He sighed. "Believe me, Violet, I want nothing more than to claim you in every imaginable way. But I..."

"But what? Is this because of what I told you?"

"Look, it was a lot to take in and I don't know how you thought I was going to react. I mean, I'm really sorry about everything that happened to you. Nobody deserves to go through any of that."

I jumped up from the couch and before I realized what I was saying, the words left my lips.

"You need to go!"

Grayson stood up and saddled his hands on his hips, hesitantly meeting my eyes. "Actually, that is something I was going to do, anyway."

I furrowed my brows. "What do you mean?"

His hesitance started my heart aching again.

"I'm leaving in an hour for Manhattan."

The words hit me like a sledgehammer.

"I see. And just when were you going to tell me this?"

He took a step back. "I was gonna tell you at dinner, but things didn't turn out that way."

"Sorry to ruin your plans," I huffed.

He sighed again. "Look, I've gotta leave cause I'm going on tour in March and I need to start rehearsals and get things lined up. There's a lot involved."

"You're going on tour? Where does that leave us?"

My eyes filled up again as the words crossed my lips in a whisper. I needed to know.

"Or is there a *US*?"

My question hung heavy in the air as he stood quietly and alternated between staring at me and the floor.

"Damn it Grayson! Answer me! Is there something between us or was I just another way for you to pass the time? Another notch on your guitar case?"

His lack of response gave me my answer.

He looked at me one last time before he turned and started out of the room. The beautiful eyes that I looked to for light and love were now dark and cold. I stormed up behind him and slammed my fist into his back.

"You son of a bitch! You're just like every other man! I wish I had never met you and wasted my time on you! Get the fuck out of my house and don't EVER come back!"

He shrugged his shoulders and walked to the front door, pausing as he opened it. His voice was quiet and low.

"I'm sorry."

And with that, Grayson Maddox walked out my door and out of my life.

As I gasped for air, my lungs burned and I collapsed to the floor. My body crumpled into a ball and my heavy sobs returned. My mind tried to process the finality.

This time... he wasn't chasing after me.

This time... he wasn't coming back.

This time I knew... it was really over.

CHAPTER NINETEEN

The next five days were an agonizing hell. Every second of the day, I had to force myself to breathe. I wasn't living; I was existing. Existing in a world without him. And I didn't know how to continue. Our breakup was just as fast and sudden as our attraction. I should have known better than to allow myself to get involved with him.

But I did. Maybe I *was* a groupie.

He wanted my honesty, and I gave it to him. I took a chance and lowered my walls... my defenses... not for Grayson Maddox, the superstar, but for Mr. Bertram, the man. Hell, I didn't even know his real first name. I hated him for breaking my heart. But I hated myself more for allowing him to do it. I hated myself for thinking that I was different from any other woman he had been with. My appetite was non-existent and the only sleep I got came from the exhaustion of all my crying. The silence of the house was almost deafening, save for the ticking of the clock on my kitchen wall. I would stare at the door, reliving the moment he walked out over and over again, silently wishing that he would come sweeping back in and tell me he was wrong.

But by the fourth day, I knew that would never happen. I was going to have to learn how to move on, no matter how hard it was. The golden globe in the sky rose just like it had each previous day, and I forced myself to climb out of bed. I threw on some sweatpants and a t-shirt and looked at myself in the mirror on the closet door. The pale hue blanketing my face, bloodshot eyes, and heavy bags now sitting on the apples of my cheeks were an outward reflection of my inner turmoil. As much as I wanted to just lie back down and pull the covers over my head, I rejoined civilization, even if only for a little while. I donned my feet with a pair of flats, made my way downstairs and staggered out the door into the late morning rays. Slipping on a pair of sunglasses, I walked to my car and jumped in, deciding on a trip to the mall for some retail therapy.

After relishing in the warm buttery taste of a pretzel from Hot Sam's, I walked over to Lerner's and bought a couple pairs of jeans and some tops. As I came out of the store, on my way to pick up a new pair of boots, I spotted something that snapped my head to attention. There in the food court, basking in the orange neon glow of the Burger King sign, was none other than Biff. But it wasn't Buffy he was with. It was Dottie. They looked to be very lovey dovey with each other. He was playfully tapping her on the nose while she was smiling and laughing. I stood and watched them until they got up from their table. And since I had nothing else better to do, I followed them. It actually turned my stomach to watch them holding hands. I felt bad for Buffy.

They walked into Sears, and I continued behind them, keeping my distance. We walked through the garden and shoe departments, eventually ending up in ladies' lingerie. I stood back in the corner by the dressing rooms and watched as Biff picked out different nightgowns, telling Dottie how sexy she would look in them. Now I was ready to puke. The last one he picked out was a pretty blue see through one. The color made me think of Grayson. I imagined him and me in Biff and Dottie's place. The pain in my heart knocked again, and my eyes misted over. And before I realized it, an audible sob slipped out. Biff and Dottie whipped around and looked at me like a deer caught in headlights.

"Oh, shit!" Dottie exclaimed before her old wrinkled ass ran off toward electronics. Biff stalked toward me and I turned to duck into a room, but they were all locked. There was nowhere I could go.

"Violet! What the hell are you doing here? How long have you been standing there?"

I was not in the mood for his bullshit, and I wouldn't back down. I looked up at his fake tanned face. "Long enough!"

I tried to walk away, but everywhere I stepped, he would step, blocking my path.

"You will forget what you saw today. And if you don't," his tone was low and menacing, "I won't be responsible for what happens."

"Is that a threat?" I was ready to beat his ass with my shopping bags if he tried anything.

Biff glowered at me. "Just mind your own damn business if you know what's good for you." With a final huff, he stormed away, calling for Dottie. He had some nerve threatening me. I had the mind to go call Buffy. But as much as she needed to know, I couldn't be the cause of someone else's heartache.

I left Sears and headed out of the mall, keeping a wary eye out for Biff or Dottie. I climbed in my Firebird and headed back home. After clipping the tags off my new clothes and hanging them in the closet, I laid down to take a nap. About two hours later, I roused up and headed downstairs to fix something to eat. I still didn't have much of an appetite, but I didn't want to die from starvation. After my dinner date with Chef Boyardee, I grabbed a bottle of wine from the cupboard and went back upstairs to soak in a nice, long bath.

An hour and a half bottle later, I pulled my wrinkled, lobster-colored body out of the tub. I rummaged through the dresser and my eyes settled on the cream-colored satin nightgown. I purchased it a long time ago after seeing it in a lingerie shop and falling in love with the delicate lace trim. For some reason, I never wore it. But when I met Grayson, I knew I wanted to wear it the night we made love for the first time. I had no reason to save it now. I lifted my arms and smoothed the soft fabric over my slightly damp body and sighed. My thoughts swirled around in my head on an endless loop. Biff and Dottie, poor Buffy, what I was going to do about my job, my mom, and, of course, Mr. Maddox. I pulled the plush comforter back and climbed into bed, reaching to turn off the lamp. My heavy lids fell shut, and I soon drifted off to dreamland.

***

A sudden loud banging noise jerked me from my slumber. I rolled over and listened.

There was nothing.

My mind was playing tricks on me.

I rolled back over and closed my eyes, snuggling closer to my pillow.

I heard it again. It sounded like a knock on the door.

KNOCK KNOCK

Someone was knocking. I sat up and switched the light on, looking at my clock. It was after midnight. Who in the hell was at my door at this hour? For a split second, I thought back to what Biff said. I hoped he wasn't dumb enough to come here and start some shit.

KNOCK KNOCK KNOCK

The pounding on my door continued.

Damn, who died? It's not that serious! I jumped out of bed and hurried down the stairs. Whoever it was had better have an excellent reason for waking me up. I got to the last step and switched on the lamp before answering the door. I loosened the deadbolt on the top, turned the lock on the knob, and jerked the door open.

"WHAT?!"

A familiar pair of hazel eyes waited on the other side.

In one swift motion, he pushed me back and stepped inside, kicking the door shut behind him. His powerful hands grasped my waist and spun me around, slamming me up against the back of the door. Pressing his firm physique and semi-hard cock against my satin covered body, his hungry eyes stalked me like a lion ready to pounce on its prey. I opened my mouth to speak, but his plump pink lips crashed against mine, silencing me. All I could do was moan and pray that I wasn't dreaming. My hands feasted on his body before tangling in his hair. I lifted my leg and wrapped it around his waist, pulling him closer to the heat now radiating from the soft spot between my legs. His familiar hands roamed the soft curves of my body. I melted into his touch. It had only been four days. Four long days.

His soft lips broke away from mine and moved to whisper against my ear. "I've been bad, Violet," he moaned, his heady breath prickling my skin.

He reached for the right strap of my nightgown and smoothed it down my shoulder, exposing my breast. "And I want you," his lips trailed a fiery blaze down my neck, "to show me..." He kissed my shoulder, then enveloped my breast with his hot mouth, sucking gently on my dusky nipple.

My brain swam with delirium as little waves of electrical impulses coursed through my body. "Show you... what?" I held him like a child at its mother's bosom.

His slick tongue swirled around my breast one last time before he lifted his head, his dark lust-filled eyes meeting mine again. The words he spoke next came as pure shock.

"How you punish a bad boy..."

The seriousness of his face reeled me in. If he wanted to play the game, I was more than willing and happy to oblige.

I moved my lips next to his ear, nibbling and licking his earlobe as I whispered my response.

"Take me upstairs."

CHAPTER TWENTY

Grayson gently lifted me up, and I instinctively wrapped my legs around his waist, while my arms linked around his neck. No words needed to be spoken as he carried me up the stairs. The glances of desire and anticipation in our eyes were more than enough. When we reached the landing, I unwrapped myself from him and intertwined our fingers, leading him down the hallway, stopping outside of my bedroom.

I brushed his lips with a soft kiss. "I'll be right back."

I walked into my bedroom, opened the closet, and reached for the black box. Tearing off the lid, I grabbed for the key buried inside. I quickly returned to him and reconnected our hands. We continued our journey down the hallway, coming to a stop in front of my spare bedroom. I placed the small bronze key in the lock and turned it. The clicking of the tumblers echoed in the surrounding stillness.

"Are you sure you want to do this?" My eyes met his, searching for any sign of doubt or hesitation. There wasn't any. I just hoped that he understood what was about to happen. Once we entered that room, there was no turning back.

His response was low but confident. "Yes."

That was all I needed to hear. I opened the door and led him inside. The room was dark, but I knew it like the back of my hand. I guided him to the middle and pushed him down onto a large metal chair.

"Don't move! If you do, there will be hell to pay!"

I turned away from him and left the room, slamming the door behind me. I ran back to my bedroom, stripped off my satin nightgown and reached inside the box again. I removed the black leather corset and smoothed my fingers across it. It had been so long since I had worn it. I loosened the zipper on the front and slipped it on, the cool soft leather enveloping my skin felt heavenly. It fit like a glove. I zipped it back up and adjusted the top, pushing up my breasts until they almost spilled out. My hands returned to the box and produced a black leather thong, with a pair of black fingerless gloves. Lifting my feet one at a time, I glided the panties up my legs to rest firmly against my quickly dampening mound. I then slipped on the gloves and tightened the Velcro straps. All that remained were my boots. I removed them from the box and slipped on the six inch heeled shoes one at a time, pulling the little metal zipper resting at my ankle to the middle of my thighs. After buckling the two belts at the top of each boot,

I looked at myself in the closet mirror. I looked damn good. My body shivered with anticipation. Poor Grayson didn't know what he was getting into. There was only one more thing I needed. I returned to the box for the last time and removed the pièce de résistance — my whip. It was the first piece of equipment I ever bought. It was black, and I absolutely loved the purple rose that adorned the end of the handle. I walked to the doorway, flipped my hair back, and took a deep breath. Violet Deveraux was gone. Mistress Crimson was now in charge

The click of my stiletto boots echoed on the hardwood floor as I returned to the room. I jerked the door open, confidently walked inside, and slammed it shut.

Let the fun begin!

"About time you came back. I was wondering when —"

"Shut the fuck up!"

Grayson quickly closed his mouth. After grabbing an item from the cabinet in the corner, I walked over to the switch on the wall and flipped it on. The room filled with a red hue and the music system kicked on, playing dark, bass filled dance music. I watched as he looked around the room, his eyes drinking in the sight.

"You aren't the only one who loves red."

I sauntered over to stand in front of him. He looked me up and down and attempted to speak again.

"Damn baby! You look fine as fuck!"

I reared my hand back and smacked him across the face.

"I told you to shut up!"

Grayson slowly turned back to face me, still reeling from the sudden unexpected slap, his hand rubbing his jaw, his eyes full of shock and disbelief.

"That's better."

I paced a circle around the chair, watching him, smoothing the ends of the whip through my fingers as I spoke.

"Grayson Maddox... the musical genius... loved and hated by people all around the world... the wild, bad boy who commands the stage with his presence and his words. The man whose sex appeal has women falling at his feet everywhere he goes. The man who is now..." I stopped pacing and was now standing behind him. I lovingly draped the spiked leather collar around his brawny neck, loving the sound of it snapping shut. Lowering my lips beside his ear, I whispered in a heady breath. "My bitch!"

Grayson flinched in the chair and swallowed hard, his hands tugging at the rough tightness encasing his throat.

"Now, before we begin with your lesson, we need to establish some ground rules. You will refer to me as Mistress or Mistress Crimson. You will ask permission for everything you do, even to come, and you will thank me afterward. The collar around your neck represents your position as my chosen pet. Your only purpose is to please me. If you don't, the punishment I bestow upon you will be harsh. If you feel the need to stop, we will use a safety word. I will allow you to choose this word. You may speak now."

Grayson hesitated for a moment. "Banana." His voice was low and barely audible.

"I can't hear you! Speak up!"

He raised his voice. "My safety word is Banana."

I threw my head back and roared with laughter. "Banana? What the hell does that mean?"

"It was my nickname as a kid." he mumbled, lowering his head.

I tapped a long red painted nail against my chin. "Interesting. Well, Chiquita, let's begin. I want you to strip!" Grayson's beautiful hazel eyes locked with mine as he slowly stood up and lifted his black t-shirt over his head, laying it on the chair. I raised my whip and cracked it across his hands and bare chest.

WHACK

"What the fuck was that for?"

I smacked him again.

WHACK

"You didn't ask my permission to remove your clothes. Now try again!"

His shaky hands reached for the button at the top of his jeans, then stopped. "Mistress, may I remove my pants?"

A devilish smile curled my lips. "Very good. Yes, you may."

He undid the button and zipper, slid them down his long hairy legs, over his black boots, and stepped out of them. His semi-hard cock sprung out for my viewing pleasure. I wanted it buried deep inside of me so badly that I had to bite my lip to stay in character.

"Thank you, Mistress."

I nodded my head in approval. "You learn fast. But, I'm still punishing you for not wearing any underwear. Now, take off your boots."

Grayson shook his head. "No, Mistress, I won't take off my boots."

I tapped the whip against my hand. "Yes, you will or else!"

He lowered his head as he reluctantly lifted one leg at a time and removed his boots. He wasn't wearing socks, and I noticed some scars across the tops of each one. I wondered how they got there.

I placed my finger under his chin and lifted his dark eyes back to mine. "You have beautiful feet Pet, never be ashamed of them."

"Thank you, Mistress." A small smile sat on his plump lips.

I lowered my hand and teasingly caressed his cock with my gloved hand. He shivered beneath my touch. "You like that, Pet?"

"Yes Mistress, I do."

I continued smoothing my hand back and forth along his length, increasing my speed. Grayson screwed his eyes shut and his head fell back as a slight moan left his lips.

"Mistress, that feels so good." His breathing picked up in intensity. "Mistress, may I ask a question?"

"Yes, Pet, you may."

"Will Mistress please suck my dick?"

I stopped and jerked my hand away.

"NO! Mistress will not suck your dick! You are to do as *I* say and please!" Oh, he was in for it now. "Get your ass down on all fours and crawl over to the sex bench! And I want you to bark like a dog as you do it!"

His brown orbs reluctantly linked with mine as he lowered his body to the floor, getting on all fours.

"I can't hear you, Pet!"

A mumbling sound came from the floor.

I placed the pointed heel of my boot against his ass and shoved him. "Louder!"

"Woof"

"DAMN IT, I SAID LOUDER!"

"WOOF! WOOF!"

I watched as one of the greatest superstars of all time crawled across the floor and barked like a dog. The realization of the power that I now held over him made me giddy. I placed a hand over my mouth to keep a laugh from escaping. He reached the black leather bench and took his position, bending over it, his ass perched high in the air.

"You have disobeyed me, Pet, by asking me to suck your dick. And for that, you must pay!"

CHAPTER TWENTY-ONE

I walked to the small cabinet in the corner and grabbed a bottle of lube, a new piece of equipment, and a surprise. Grayson snapped his head in my direction and watched as I perched myself behind him.

"Oh, hell no Violet! You ain't stickin' ANYTHING in MY ass!"

The cold metal of the spiked riding crop cracked against his back.

WHACK WHACK

"OW! SHIT!"

"I told you, Pet, when you don't follow the rules, there is hell to pay. Now, you wanna try that last part again?"

He blew out a long, unsteady breath. "Sorry, Mistress."

I placed my hands on his ass and parted his soft dimpled cheeks, lightly running a finger around his little puckered star. "Relax Pet, it will be uncomfortable at first, but you will soon feel pleasure." I grabbed the bottle of lube and squirted some down his crack and smoothed it around his hole, slowly inserting the surprise I had for him.

"FUCK!" he screamed, jerking up off the bench, his fists banging out a disorganized concerto. "Mistress! What the hell is that?!"

I reached for the 'on' switch and flipped it. Grayson writhed against the bench even more.

I laughed. "That, my Pet, is a vibrating anal plug. The vibrating helps stimulate your prostate gland, causing more intense orgasms. Stop moving around. It will make it hurt worse." I reached for the other button on the device that controlled the intensity and turned it all the way up.

He moaned even louder.

I walked to the front of the bench and saw the painful look twisted on his face. In some small way, it made me happy. Now, maybe he knew the pain my heart felt when he walked out.

"Mistress, please stop and take it out!"

Looking into his desperate eyes, I whispered ever so softly, "No." I walked halfway back down the bench and reached underneath of him, latching onto his cock, stroking him as he whimpered in pain. It didn't take long for him to harden in my hand. But he wasn't getting off that easily. I let go of him and returned to the end of the bench. Wrapping my fingers around the anal plug, I yanked it out. Grayson's agonizing screams of pain echoed off the walls, almost drowning out the music. I was sure that he had never hit that high note on stage.

"GET DOWN!"

He slowly backed up and climbed down off the bench.

"GET ON THE BED!"

His mist filled eyes conveyed what his voice pleaded. "Please Mistress, no more."

"Aww poor baby, boo hoo. What do you think all your fans would say if they saw you right now? Hmm? You're a pussy, Grayson Maddox! Now get on the fucking bed!"

He lowered his head and gingerly walked over to the bed, climbing on it. As soon as he was in position, I reached for the restraints attached to the spiked headboard and latched the metal cuffs around his wrists. Moving to the foot of the bed, I attached another set to his ankles. He looked so helpless... so fragile... so fuckable. I grabbed something from the table by the bed before climbing on and straddling myself over his thighs. I took hold of his dick again and pumped the meaty piece of flesh. His hazel eyes locked with mine. "Your cock is so beautiful, Pet."

His voice was raspy and weak. "Thank you, Mistress."

I continued to stroke him. He was so hard he could have jackhammered through a wall. His head was thrown back, his eyes were tightly shut, and his breathing was labored.

"But you know something, Pet, it's a shame that your cock has been in so many pussies..." I lowered the metal ball clamp over his penis and down around his delicate jewels, tightening the screws, "except the most important one."

Grayson's eyes snapped opened, and they were full of fear. He looked down at the device now adorning him.

"Wha... what is that, Mistress?"

I bent over and lowered my face to his. "Payback."

I resumed stroking him and his cries of agony became louder and longer. A faint stream of tears were slowly sliding down his face. He begged and pleaded with me. "Please, Mistress, can I come? I need to come... it hurts so bad!"

My answer was always the same. "NO!"

I stopped stroking him and carefully inched my body up toward the head of the bed, now straddling his chest. My fingers latched onto the lace of my thong and pulled it to the side.

"Why don't you want my pussy, Pet?" I slid a finger inside my wetness and coated it. "It wants you." I ran the slickness across Grayson's lips. As he sucked it into his mouth and licked it, I started rubbing my crotch against him. "But, it's ok Pet, if you don't want my pussy... cause there are a lot of other men who have had it... and still want it!"

If looks could have killed, I would have been dead. The look on Mr. Maddox's face actually scared me.

"Violet, I'm done playin'. If you don't let me out of this shit, so help me..."

"Aww, what's wrong... baby, don't want to play anymore?"

The bed violently shook as Grayson jerked against the restraints. I was afraid he would actually break the headboard. "Damn it Violet, I'm serious. You better fuckin' let me go!"

The seriousness of his tone told me he was pissed, and playtime was definitely over. So I let him go. I climbed off of him and moved to remove the ball clamp and loosen the cuffs around his ankles. I then returned to the headboard to loosen the ones on his wrists. As soon as the last cuff fell off, he jumped up from the bed and, in one fell swoop, he threw me down onto it. Grabbing my arms, he tightened the cuffs around my wrists.

"Hey! What the hell you doin'? This wasn't part of the plan!"

Grayson quickly climbed on top of me, supporting his weight on his arms and hands. Lowering his face mere inches from mine, his long locks created our own private curtain. His voice was deep and menacing.

"You will NEVER let another man come near you or touch you. Do you understand?"

My mouth opened to respond, but he placed his hand over it.

"I don't give a fuck if you do or you don't understand. I'm the *only* man who will EVER be in your bed from now on!"

Our eyes hungered for each other. The want and need was so raw at that moment, it poured from both of us. Grayson reached for my corset and jerked the zipper down, letting my heavy breasts spill free. Grabbing for my thong, he ripped it from my body, throwing it across the room. He sat back and his slender fingers dug into the flesh of my thighs, spreading them, positioning himself at my entrance.

"You're mine Violet," he growled. "ALL MINE!"

And with those words, he plunged deep into my core. His lips forcefully crashed against mine, sucking the air from my lungs. He lifted my legs and spread them wider. I whimpered and moaned against him as he controlled me. He was like a wildman, fucking me hard and fast, his cock pushing deeper with each thrust. I could feel him pounding against my cervix. I closed my eyes, but he demanded me to stop.

"No! You look at me Violet! I wanna watch you come!"

I was almost there and I could tell he was, too. He was thrusting so forcefully that the bed was moving across the floor.

"Uhh... ohhh Grayson... I'm almost... almost..."

"Don't call me that... call me by my real name."

"What... what's that?"

"Eugene."

I was on the verge of blacking out and I barely comprehended what he had said.

"Oh... Eugene!"

Grayson smiled like the Cheshire cat. "Come for me baby... show me everything."

With one last thrust, the gates to Shangri-La burst open and I fell over the edge. I still locked my eyes with his as my body shook and my slick walls continued to spasm, milking his cock, finally pushing him toward his crescendo.

"UHHH FUCK... VIOLETTTT!!!!"

I felt his warm seed spray against my womb. His release was so intense, so animalistic, that he almost roared. After a few more spasms, he climbed off me and collapsed on the bed. We both lay there, trying to catch our breath, basking in the afterglow. My arms were aching from being in the cuffs and he must have noticed my discomfort, so he got up and released the locks. There was a small tickle of blood running down my right arm from where the metal had cut into it. He brought my wrist to his mouth and sucked the tangy residue from it before trailing his tongue down my arm to collect the rest. The entire act was so sweet, so erotic. As he did this, my brain recovered from the recent flow of dopamine and a stark realization set in.

"You didn't pull out."

He smirked and chuckled lightly. "I was marking my territory." The uncertainty in my eyes must have concerned him. "Are you worried?"

I sat quietly for a moment before answering him. "No, never with you." I skimmed my hand down the side of his beautiful face. "Why did you come back?"

He gathered my hands in his and locked his eyes with mine. "Honestly, I missed you. When I got back home, all I could do was think about you. And... I was curious."

As much as I wanted to tell him how badly he hurt me when he left, and how he broke my heart, I left it alone for now so we could enjoy the time we had together. "Well, how was it?" A small laugh left my lips.

His face was unreadable. "It was different. But mostly, I liked it. Except for that anal plug. I didn't like that shit. But this right here," he smoothed his fingers across the collar around his neck, "I dig this!"

Grayson was very sexy with the collar on. I teasingly scoffed at him. "And I took it easy on you!"

We both roared with laughter.

"Look, I know I have to leave soon."

My laugh quickly died out. My heart could not go through any more pain with him.

"But I want us to spend as much time as we can together."

I swallowed hard and looked at him. "And how do we do that?"

A huge grin lit up his face. "I want you to come back to Manhattan with me, to Maddox Manor. I wanna show you *my* world. I want you with me."

"Maddox Manor?"

A genuine laugh escaped him. "Yeah, Maddox Manor is the name of my home. Like Elvis has Graceland."

I nodded in understanding. "Oh, ok."

My dark lover lay down across the bed and pulled me against him, his long arms enveloping my body, his lips brushing light kisses against my skin as he spoke.

"I have to leave in the morning but I want you to think about it, ok?"

I turned my head toward him, meeting his sincere gaze. "Ok, I will... Eugene. Ya know we have to talk about that, right?"

He smiled as we shared a passionate kiss before I rolled over and snuggled closer to him. Not long after, sleep claimed both of our weary bodies.

CHAPTER TWENTY-TWO

A few hours later, I roused from my slumber. As my eyes fluttered open, I released a loud yawn and stretched. A smile spread across my face as the events of only a short time ago played in my mind. I still couldn't believe that Grayson allowed me to use him the way I had. He was always the dominate one. Grayson! Oh shit! My mind snapped to full attention as I rolled over to face the other side of the bed.

He was gone.

A twinge of pain pricked my heart.

I noticed a piece of paper lying on the table next to the bed and reached for it.

I wanted to laugh and cry all at the same time as I skimmed the note he left behind. He always had a way with words. I wanted to go to him, but still wasn't a hundred percent sure. This would be a big step for me. I had never been on an airplane, let alone traveled to another state. And what would happen once I was there? I was not a superstar like Grayson Maddox, and I didn't know how I would fit into his world. I would be myself, but would that be good enough? He and I needed to sit down and talk about what we both expected from each other and from this relationship. Yes, I referred to it now as a relationship. I was not another one of his groupies, who he could just fuck, then walk away.

He was definitely all man, and I knew he always wanted to be the one in charge, but last night I sensed an almost childlike vulnerability in him I don't think most people saw. It had to be hard for him to always be 'on' for the public while trying to keep some sense of privacy and not lose his mind while doing it. He had also been revealing glimpses here and there into his past and it made me think that deep down, we really weren't that different.

I climbed out of bed and winced at the dull ache between my legs. Grayson was a tall man and as funny as it sounded, he sure fit that adage about tall men with big feet. With the paper nestled in my hand, I headed back to my bedroom, locking the door to the playroom behind me. Walking into my room, I headed straight to the bathroom, turning on the shower to a nice, hot temperature. I climbed in and let the water run over my sore muscles, relaxing me. After I showered and got dressed, I went downstairs to the kitchen and fixed some breakfast. Awesome sex sure worked up my appetite. As I ate, my thoughts swirled around again in my head. I only had one week left on my suspension from work. And honestly, I really didn't know if I wanted to go back. I needed the money, but I would not compromise myself anymore. I had been through enough in my life. And I just couldn't stomach the thought of facing Biff and Dottie again. I needed to decide what I was going to do, and soon.

However, right now, I had a bigger decision to make. As I finished my oatmeal, I thought about my mom and the last time we spoke. She was right when she said that it was time for me to take a chance and try to love again. I just prayed that this time, Grayson wouldn't break my heart like he did before. Throwing caution and perhaps my sanity to the wind, I made my decision. I got up from the table, put my bowl in the sink and walked over to the phone, my fingers shaking as I held the paper and dialed the number. On the third ring, a voice answered.

"Hello, this is Robbie Hauck, Mr. Maddox's personal assistant. How can I help you?"

My mouth opened and produced a squeak.

"Hello? Is anyone there?"

I quickly found my voice. "Uh yes, I'm here."

"How can I help you?"

"M-my name is Violet… Violet Deveraux."

"Ah yes, Mr. Maddox told me you would be calling."

How the hell did he know I would call?

A nervous laugh tinged my voice. "Yes, well, he gave me this number and here I am."

"No need to worry, Ms. Deveraux, I will have everything arranged."

"Arranged?"

"Yes, Mr. Maddox explained to me you are to meet him here in Manhattan for some business meetings."

Business meetings? Seriously?

"Once I've completed everything, I will call you back. Can you please provide me with your phone number?"

My mind was going into overdrive. This was really going to happen.

"Ms. Deveraux? Are you still there?"

"Uh yeah, I'm still here. My phone number is 312-555-0377."

"Ok, I got it. You can expect my call in the next few hours. I'll talk to you soon. Enjoy your day!"

"Thanks Robbie and you too."

I hung up the phone and sat back down at the kitchen table. What did I just get myself into?

***

I was in the middle of cutting up some tomatoes for a salad to go with my spaghetti dinner when the phone rang.

"Hello?"

"Ms. Deveraux, this is Robbie Hauck."

"Yes, hello."

"I wanted to let you know everything is ready for your trip here to Manhattan."

My stomach became fast friends with my feet.

"A car will pick you up at 7:00am tomorrow morning and take you to O'Hare International. At 9:45am you will board United Airlines flight 777 to Manhattan. You will arrive here at LaGuardia Airport around 11:30am and there will be a driver waiting for you. He will collect your luggage, then bring you to Maddox Manor. Mr. Maddox will not be here when you arrive, but I will, and I will make sure you get settled. Do you have any questions for me?"

"No, I think I'm good. I took notes. Thank you for all your help, Robbie."

I could hear the smile in his voice. "You're very welcome. Have a safe flight and I look forward to meeting you!"

"Thank you. Goodbye."

"Goodbye!"

And with that, it was official. I was totally crazy, and I was on my way to New York.

***

After finishing my dinner, I called my next-door neighbor Mildred and explained to her I would be leaving for a couple of days and asked if she would keep an eye on my place. She gladly obliged. I was lucky to have such friendly neighbors. I went upstairs to pack for my 'business meetings'. Opening the closet, I pulled out my Ricardo of Beverly Hills luggage. Tres chic. Picking up the largest piece, I laid it on the bed, unzipped it, and looked inside. What the hell was I supposed to pack? I knew nothing about New York except it was cold, it snowed a lot, and there were lots of muggers. But it was still fall, and I hoped the weather would be nice. Plus, I didn't know how to dress around Grayson. Sure, I had my office clothes, which were nice, and then there were always sweat pants and t-shirts, but what else does one wear around a musical superstar and his friends? I packed the only clothes I had and hoped they'd be acceptable. Next, I gathered up my personal items from the bathroom and put them in the smaller suitcase. I then returned to my closet and grabbed for my shoes, stuffing them in the last bag.

I zipped up the bags and sat them by my bedroom door. I had to be ready at seven, so I climbed into bed early. Turning off the light, I laid there in the dark, staring at the ceiling. My mind was racing at a million miles an hour. What was this trip going to be like? What was our time together going to be like? I finally wore myself out from all my overthinking, so I pulled the comforter up over me and my eyes drifted shut.

CHAPTER TWENTY-THREE

The blaring of my alarm clock at six o'clock jolted me from my slumber. I rolled over, slammed my hand against the off button, and untangled myself from the comforter. Today was the day. I tossed my legs over the side of the bed, stretched towards the heavens, then headed for the bathroom. After taking care of business and a quick shower, I shimmied into a new pair of black jeans, pulled on the new purple lace top I had bought, and slipped on my black suede boots with fringe on the side. As I brushed my hair, I studied myself in the closet mirror and gave myself a pep talk. I was excited yet nervous, but I was ready to do this. I just hoped Grayson was, too.

After one last look, I grabbed for my luggage and drug it down the steps. It was only a few bags, but damn, it was heavy. It felt like I had packed a dead body. Thank God the big piece had wheels on it. I sat the group by the front door, then went in the kitchen to grab a snack. My stomach was already in knots and I really wasn't hungry, but I didn't want to get nauseous on the flight. The house was eerily quiet as I ate my rice cakes. Each munch echoed off the walls. As I took the last bite of the second cake, there was a loud knock at the front door. I walked over and opened it.

"Good Morning Miss!" a gray-headed, stocky man in a nice suit and cap exclaimed from the other side. "My name is Paul and I will be your driver today."

I flashed him a small smile. "Good morning Paul."

He looked around me and motioned to my luggage. "Is this all you have?"

I nodded. "Yes, it's only three pieces."

He took the bags, and I thanked him.

"You're welcome. Now, if you'll follow me to the car, we will be on our way."

I returned to the kitchen and picked up my purse from the table. Walking back to the living room, I took one last look around the house and said a silent goodbye before heading out the door. I followed Paul outside to a black Cadillac and waited as he put my luggage in the trunk. He then opened the back door and helped me in. A few seconds later, he was climbing into the front seat. As we pulled away from the curb, I looked out the tinted window at my house. I would see it again in a week. But how I would be when I returned, I didn't know. My emotions were all over the place as of late, and I needed to get myself together. I turned to face the console in front of me and wrapped my fingers around the small gray knob there, adjusting the air conditioning. As the cool air wafted over me, I laid my head back against the leather headrest and drifted asleep.

***

A light tapping on my shoulder stirred me to life. I opened my eyes and Paul was standing next to me. "We have arrived, Miss."

"Thank you, Paul." I yawned, trying to stretch out the slight kink in my neck.

I placed my hand in his, and he helped me out of the car. After retrieving my luggage, we entered through the doors of O'Hare International. As Paul spoke with a skycap about checking in my bags, I walked around and took in the busy atmosphere of the terminal. So many people with so many stories. I wondered if any of them would be on my flight.

When Paul finished his conversation, he walked back over and handed me a piece of paper and something green. "Miss, it has been a pleasure driving for you today. Is there anything else you need?"

I looked down at what he handed me. It was my boarding pass plus a hundred-dollar bill. I was confused. "No, I don't think I need anything. But what is this money for?"

"I was told by my boss that the man arranging this trip wanted you to have some money in case you needed anything before you arrived."

Grayson was so thoughtful. My heart warmed, and the feeling radiated up my face, producing a smile on my lips.

"If there is nothing else, I will be on my way."

"No, there is nothing else. Thank you Paul for everything."

He tipped his hat at me. "You're welcome Miss. Safe travels."

I strolled through the terminal until I reached the arrival and departure board. My eyes scanned the huge listing until they settled on flight 777. I would leave from gate E13. Looking up at the sign directly overhead, I saw I was only at gate D11. I still had a way to go. As I walked,

I glanced at all the people and all the different shops that were around. There were coffee places, food places, even shopping places. After what felt like a ten-mile walk, I finally rounded the corner to gate E13. My eyes widened as I suddenly noticed the best place of all. A music store.

"Good morning," a friendly voice called out as I entered Tommy's Terrific Tunes.

"Hello."

A tall, slender man approached me. "Is there anything I can help you with today?"

"Not really, I'm just looking."

"Ok, well let me know if you need any anything."

I walked up and down the aisles, thumbing through the albums, checking out the latest from Bon Jovi, then moving down to Motley Crue. I neared the end of the stack for Poison and stopped at the next plastic card in front of me — Rancid Orchid. I took my time reading each cover and stopped when I came to one that featured Grayson in all his bad boy glory on the front. The album was called 'Loverman' and I couldn't tear my eyes away from it. He was beautiful. He looked so raw... so primal. After our last encounter, I knew just how primal he could be. I grabbed the record and headed to the register.

"Rancid Orchid, huh? You a fan?"

I smirked at the young pimply-faced kid behind the register. "I guess you could say that."

He rang up my purchase. "That will be $10.12."

I handed him the hundred-dollar bill. He placed the record in a bag and handed me both the bag and my change.

"You know, they helped produce the soundtrack to the Batman movie a couple of years ago."

"Really?"

"Yeah, and the singer dated the lead actress, too. Carolyne Bernard. Man, she is one fine chick! It lasted about a year and was a very hot affair."

My confidence plummeted to the floor. I was sure Grayson had dated his share of beautiful women over the years, but if he had dated a superstar like her, what the hell did he see, or want, in me?

"And I heard they're getting ready to go on tour in a few months."

That familiar pang in my heart returned. I already knew that, but played along. "Oh, really?"

"Yeah, I heard it's going to be called the 'Longer and Bigger' tour. I think they're touring North America and Europe this time, too."

I nodded slightly as I turned to leave. "Thanks for letting me know. I'll check into it."

"Thanks for stopping by. Have a nice day!"

As I left the store, there was an announcement over the airport intercom. "Flight 777 to Manhattan now boarding at Gate E13."

I walked back over to the waiting area and got in the boarding line. When it was my turn, I showed my pass to the attendant. "Hello and welcome to United Airlines. You will sit in Section A, Seat 2. That is in the first-class section. Please show your pass to the flight attendant when you enter the aircraft. Enjoy your flight!"

I took a deep breath and walked down the slightly shaky ramp to the plane. As I entered, I showed my pass to a bubbly flight attendant whose plastic nametag announced her as Camille. She escorted me to the first-class section and told me to let her know if I needed anything. I placed my purse and bag in the overheard compartment, snapped it shut and sat down in the spacious gray seat. Grayson sure went out of his way for this trip. I had to make sure I thanked him properly. The overhead speaker crackled and a deep male voice, who announced himself as the captain, told us to pay attention to the flight attendants as they went over the safety rules.

After they finished, he announced they had cleared us for takeoff. I buckled my seatbelt and took a deep breath, praying I didn't pass out. The roar of the engines sounded beneath me and the plane slowly taxied down the runway. I turned my head to look out the little window that was next to me. We came to a momentary standstill, then moved again. I watched as the world suddenly went from zero to a thousand miles an hour and we lifted off the ground. I could feel the pressure pushing against my body as we continued to climb higher into the air. A wave of nausea hit me and my head spun, so I laid back against the seat and closed my eyes.

It wasn't long before the captain was back on the intercom announcing that we had reached our cruising altitude and we were free to move around. I opened my eyes and leaned forward, looking out the window again. I marveled at the soothing blueness of the sky and the white wispy clouds that floated by, wondering if that was what Heaven was like. Turning away from the window, I looked around the plane. A golden hue from the sun's early rays bathed the entire cabin, and the only noise that existed in the calmness was the hum of the engines.

My thoughts turned to Grayson. What was he really like? What made him tick? I felt like there was more beneath the surface than what I saw. But then I thought about what the record store guy had just told me. I knew he was going on tour, but I didn't know it was to Europe, too. Would I ever see him? And if so, when? I decided I needed to make the most of the time I had with him. In the midst of my musing, Camille came by to check on me and handed me my complimentary bag of peanuts and a glass of Champaign. I thought of my mom and raised my glass in a silent toast to her. Look, mom, your little girl is following her heart.

The almost two and a half hours seemed to fly by and soon the captain came back over the intercom and informed us we were making our final descent into New York and to prepare for landing. I watched as the ground came closer into view, and the plane shook as the wheels finally connected with the runway. Once we stopped, I grabbed my purse and bag from the overhead compartment and waited until most of the other passengers exited before I did the same. I walked up the ramp and into the terminal of LaGuardia Airport. I glanced around the sea of people until my eyes landed on a tall African-American man in a suit with sunglasses on. He was holding a sign that said 'Violet D.'.

I walked over to introduce myself and offered my hand to him. "Hello, I'm Violet Deveraux."

"Hello, my name is Charles and I'm a driver for Mr. Maddox," he responded, taking my hand. "I will take you to the car and then return for your luggage. Please follow me this way."

"Thank you, Charles." I said, following behind him. We walked out of the airport to a semi-isolated area where there was a black sedan waiting. "I'll be back shortly," he said as he helped me into the back seat and shut the door. About ten minutes later, he returned and placed my luggage in the trunk. The driver's door opened, and he climbed in. "We're all set Miss Deveraux. We will arrive at Maddox Manor in about forty minutes."

We pulled away from the airport and headed to the main highway. This was it. I was on my way. My nerves kicked into overdrive and I felt flush. I stared out the window for a while, watching the busy borough traffic and concrete scenery pass by. It reminded me of Chicago. After a while, I turned around and glanced up into the review mirror. Charles' eyes met mine, and I glanced away. I looked up again and his gaze was still there.

"Are you ok Miss Deveraux?"

I cleared my throat. "Uh yes, thank you."

Charles watched the road, then glanced back up into the mirror.

"He's really a nice man."

"Excuse me?"

"Mr. Maddox, he's a nice man. He has his ways, but overall he's alright. He must like you a lot."

I twisted my face in confusion. "Why do you say that?"

"Cause he is very private and doesn't invite many people to his home. Especially outsiders. But then again, you are a pretty woman, so…"

There was a moment of silence. I couldn't believe what he just said. What the hell was that supposed to mean? It sounded like he and Biff were on the same groupie wavelength. I wanted to say something, but I didn't want to cause trouble before I got started.

"Is this your first time in New York?"

I turned to look back out the window and grumbled my answer. "Yes."

"Well, you've survived living in Chicago, so you'll love it here," he chuckled. "And I'm sure Mr. Maddox will show you a good time."

Charles just needed to shut the hell up. All I wanted to do was to get to Maddox Manor and see Grayson again. The car slowed down and took an off ramp from the highway and soon we were passing a sign that said Winding Terrace Way.

"We're here Miss Deveraux." Charles announced as we pulled up to an enormous gate surrounding a black compound-looking building. "It's not much to look at from the outside, but wait till you get inside." He rolled down his window and pushed some buttons on the small metal box sitting outside of the metal gate. With a click, the gate slowly swung open, and we drove inside. We pulled up to the front door, and he parked the car. He climbed out, opened my door, and offered his hand. My eyes stared in wonder at the vast building. This was Grayson's home, and I was really here. My heart leaped with excitement and emotion filled my eyes, causing them to mist. Charles grabbed my luggage and escorted me to the main door. He pushed the little red button on the intercom and announced our arrival. A loud click sounded from the door, and Charles held it open as I stepped inside.

CHAPTER TWENTY-FOUR

The nervous pounding of my heart echoed in my ears as we entered the house. Grayson's house. I still couldn't believe that I was really there. We stepped into the foyer and all I could say was... wow. My eyes wandered around the huge open room, full of wonderment, like a child on Christmas morning. From the deep jade of the lush foliage, over to the blue and white plush furniture, down to the intricate design of the soft beige carpeting, upward to the scrolling metal railing surrounding the balcony, I absorbed it all. But the best part was the warm golden sunlight spilling through the circle skylights. And this was only one room of the house. I could only imagine what the rest of it looked like. Charles had told me to wait and soon he returned with another gentleman.

"You must be Violet! I've been looking forward to meeting you!" The stranger extended his hand towards me. "I'm Rob Hauck. Welcome to Maddox Manor."

I accepted his hand and smiled. "Hi Rob, it's nice to meet you too."

He returned my smile, then turned to Charles. "Thank you Charles, I'll take it from here."

My eyes were still wandering around the room as Rob spoke again. "I know it's a lot to take in, but you'll love it." I nodded my head absently in agreement as he reached for my luggage. "If you'll follow me, I'll show you to your room."

We walked to the back of the room to a flight of winding stairs and continued our conversation as we started up them.

"How was your flight?"

"It was ok. It was my first time on a plane and I got a little nauseated and dizzy."

Rob frowned. "Sorry to hear that. But you arrived safely, and that's all that matters. Are you feeling ok now?"

I chuckled lightly. "Well, yes, but to be honest, my nerves are getting the best of me."

Rob stopped and turned to me just as we reached the last step. "You'll be fine. Sometimes the boss's bark is worse than his bite."

I snickered inwardly. Oh, I knew all about that bite.

When we arrived at the top of the staircase, we made a left. As we walked down the hallway, my eyes took in the variety of pictures featuring the band with and without Grayson that decorated the walls. I made a mental note to myself to take the time to view each one in more detail.

"This will be your room," Rob announced as we came to a stop at the third door down. "The boss had it prepared especially for you. Matter of fact, the decorators left about an hour before you arrived."

I felt so honored that Grayson actually had the room decorated just for me sent my heart soaring. But I also felt undeserving. Rob turned the knob, and we entered the bedroom. To say it was beautiful would've been an understatement. He really went out of his way with this. I was speechless. Rob must have seen my expression as he set my luggage in the room's corner. "I know, right? It's gorgeous!"

I shook my head. "I just can't believe that he did this."

"Well, I would say that you must be something special for him to go through so much trouble."

I felt a rush of crimson blanket over my face.

"I'll be on my way now, Miss Deveraux. The boss should be back in a few hours. I'll let him know that you have arrived. If you need anything, please press the intercom button on the table by the bed."

"I will. Thanks again Rob."

I followed him to the door and pushed it shut. Walking back over to the bed, I smoothed my hand across it. The purple duvet and silk sheets were so soft and inviting. I sat down and immediately unleashed a yawn. I was tired from my flight and Rob said that Grayson wouldn't be back for a few hours, so I decided on a nap to refresh myself. Unzipping my boots and kicking them off, I swung my legs up onto the bed. I stretched out and nestled my head on one of the king-size pillows. Another yawn escaped me as I closed my eyes.

***

Ooh yeah... that feels so good baby...

His velvet tongue lapped at my pussy like a famished cat. The tingling sensation pulsated from my clit all the way to the top of my head. He skimmed his tongue around the outside of my core before plunging it deep inside. I could feel myself nearing closer to the brink. It felt wonderful. I spread my legs wider as he increased his speed, working his magic. The familiar coil in my lower belly tightened and my inner walls started quaking. His name escaped my lips in a scream as he drank my sweetness. "Grayson!"

My eyes snapped open as I jolted awake from the best dream ever. It was so vivid and felt so real.

Then I felt the end of the bed move.

I looked down to find both my jeans and panties pulled halfway down and a familiar face staring back at me. He placed one last kiss against my fleshy folds, then one on my belly as he stalked up my body. His dark eyes locked with mine, a satisfied smirk gracing his face. "Hello."

I smiled back at him. "Hello." I caressed his cheek and skimmed my fingers through his long locks. "I thought I was dreaming."

A faint chuckle left him. "It was no dream, baby. That was all pure lovin'."

I leaned forward and briefly captured his lips. "Well, it was a lovely way to wake up. Thank you. What time is it?"

He climbed over to the other side of the bed and sat up against the headboard. "I don't keep track of time. Besides, we have all the time in the world." He smiled, eyes twinkling. "How are you? How was your trip?"

I pushed myself up to join him. "Well, despite getting a little nauseous and dizzy, it was very nice. Thank you for being so generous."

He reached for my hand and meshed our fingers together. "Aww, you're welcome. Yeah, Rob told me you didn't feel well." Bringing my hand to his lips, he placed a feather-light kiss on it. "How do you feel?"

"Better since I took that nap. But now, I feel wonderful thanks to a certain someone." I winked at him.

"Good. Cause that was just a preview." He rolled over toward me and covered my lips again with his own, the intensity and desire flowing from him into me. But our make-out session was short-lived as he quickly pulled away.

"As much as I want to lie here with you, I gotta get back to rehearsal."

I cast a disappointed frown at him. "It's ok, I understand."

He smoothed his long fingers through my hair, tucking a few stray strands behind my ear. "I'll make it up to you, I promise. Look, why don't you take a shower and get comfortable, then come join me when you're done. I'll have chef prepare dinner for us."

My head bobbed in agreement. "Ok."

I got out of the bed and turned my back to it. I grasped the bottom of my top and pulled it up and over my head, tossing it onto the bed.

"What are you doing?" My dark lover questioned, a slight hitch in his tone.

"Taking a shower." I plainly responded, reaching for my jeans.

Sliding the black denim down my legs, I purposely wiggled my ass as I yanked them off and joined them with the top. I turned back around and saw the excitement dancing in Grayson's eyes, along with the now growing hard-on tenting his pants.

I lowered my voice and spoke in a breathy tone. "You know this room is beautiful. I can't believe that you had it decorated for little ol' me."

I unhooked my lace bra and slid the soft straps down my arms, dropping it to the floor. My breasts spilled free, and I watched as he bit his bottom lip, wetting it with his thick pink tongue.

"Thank you," my fingers reached for the top of my satin panties and slowly inched them the rest of the way down my legs, "for making me feel so special." Stepping out of them, I picked them up and smoothed the soft fabric against my core, coating it with my slick juices before tossing them to my spot on the bed. Grayson immediately snatched them and brought them to his nose, inhaling deeply. I returned my hand to my pussy and snuck a finger inside, splashing around in my wet pool. Smirking seductively at him, I removed my finger and placed it in my mouth, sucking it clean.

"Enjoy your rehearsal."

I sauntered across the room, never leaving his fiery gaze, and disappeared into the bathroom, locking the door. I waited for him to come knocking, but he didn't.

After finishing my shower, I returned to the bedroom and found that he was gone. I picked up my suitcases and laid them on the bed. After taking out a fresh set of clothes, I filled the dresser drawers and closet with the rest, along with my shoes. After drying off, I slipped on my clothes and ran a brush through my dark tresses. I couldn't wait to find him and watch the musical magic he so famously created. I opened the door and stepped out into the cool air of the hallway, headed toward the stairs. As my feet hit the fourth step, I heard conversation coming from below. One voice sounded like Grayson's and the other one sounded like... a woman. I didn't want to eavesdrop, but I couldn't make my legs budge, so I stood quietly as they continued.

"Look baby, what we had was fun. But that's all it was—fun."

Yep, that was definitely him.

"Come on Genie baby, I still want you. And I know you still want me. What we had was special. Let me in and I'll make it worth your while. Nobody can suck your dick as good as I do!"

Oh, hell no! Who was this bitch?! My feet moved down to the next step, and I crouched down, hoping I could see them. But I couldn't. There was a moment of silence, then I heard Grayson speak again.

"Get off me! Stop embarrassing yourself. I told you it was over. It's been over for a while. Now take your desperate ass home and don't come back!"

The mystery woman raised her voice.

"It's someone else, isn't it? You got a new bitch under you? Who is this month's flavor? You think you can just use people for whatever you want, then toss them away, Grayson Maddox? You think you can go on with your life like nothing happened? Well, I hate to tell you, but you're wrong. Dead fucking wrong! You'll see. And if you don't, I'll make you!"

"Whatever Carolyne! Now get the hell off my property before I call the cops!"

So that's who it was, Carolyne Bernard. There was more silence than I heard the slam of a door and Grayson mumble under his breath. "And don't fuckin' come back!"

I stood back up and waited a few seconds before continuing my descent. He was sitting on a couch, staring off into space, with his hands folded and his leg angrily shaking. I walked up to him and rubbed his shoulder.

"Hey baby, you alright?" I knew he wasn't.

He jumped up and walked away. "Yeah, I'm ok. Why wouldn't I be?" I could hear the agitation in his voice and see it in his eyes. He got about halfway across the room, then turned around and walked back to me, grabbing my hand.

"Come on, dinner's waiting."

He led me to a huge dining area, and we sat down to eat. He was in another world, and I could feel the anger radiating from him. And although I knew it wouldn't be the right time to bring up our relationship, after what I had just heard, I needed to know where we stood. I needed to know if my coming there was a mistake. I took a bite of my tortellini and broke the awkward tension.

"How is rehearsal going?"

Grayson stared at his garden salad. "Fine."

I took another bite of food, then a sip of wine. "Are you getting excited about the tour? What places are you going to visit?"

"Yeah." He continued to stare at the table.

I took one last bite of food and laid my fork down. I knew he wasn't in the mood, but it was now or never.

"What exactly am I to you?"

That got his attention. He lifted his head and turned to face me, his soulful eyes staring deeply into mine.

"What is it we have? I think it's a relationship, but I want to know how you feel. I care deeply for you and I've told you that before. But how do you feel about me?" I paused for a moment, then continued. "Was my coming here a mistake?"

The agitated look reappeared on his face, but this time, it was mixed with anguish. He jumped up from the table and grabbed my arm, jerking me out of my chair.

"Ya know, I just realized that I haven't given you a proper tour of the house."

CHAPTER TWENTY-FIVE

I looked at him like he had lost his mind. Was this how he dealt with being confronted? Or how he dealt with his feelings? To just simply change the subject? I tried to keep up with him as we zoomed from the dining room back to the foyer. He paused and pointed up to the windows in the overhang by the door, placing a finger to his lips.

"Shh... listen... do you hear it?"

I tilted my head and heard the faint whooping sound of... a bird?

"Look up. That's my Victoria Crowned Pigeon."

I cast my eyes upward and sure enough, perched on a rafter was the most gorgeous bird I had ever seen. French blue feathers, a dark mask, and a maroon breast covered most of its body. A lighter shade of blue with a crest of dark blue lace with vivid white tips decorated its wings, and its eyes were a dark crimson.

"How come I didn't hear it when I first came in the door?"

Grayson shrugged his shoulders. "He was probably sleeping. He seems to be more active whenever I'm around."

"Where on Earth did you get such a beautiful animal?"

We continued to admire the bird. "He was a gift I received when we toured Australia. They are native to countries north of there. They're laid back and can live up to thirty-five years. He's usually roaming around the property, playing with Zeus."

"Wow, that's cool. He's beautiful! Does he have a name? Is Zeus another bird?"

"No, I never got around to naming him. And Zeus is my —"

Just then, the beautiful bird shit on Grayson's shoulder. "Damn it!"

All I could do was laugh at him.

"It's not funny Violet. And you'll find out who Zeus is soon enough."

As my laughter faded, things quickly took a more serious route. "Do you believe in God, Violet?" The profound seriousness of his question was clear in his eyes and tone. Where did this come from and why did he want to know?

I thought carefully before answering. "Yes Grayson, I believe in God." I paused slightly before continuing. "But sometimes, I wonder where he was when all those awful things happened to me."

We stood in silence, staring at each other for a short while before he pulled me along behind him and we continued our tour. Our next stop was to a large garage that housed his collection of vintage cars and motorcycles. It felt very surreal looking at the pieces of iconic machinery. From Corvettes to GTOs, over to Lamborghinis and Rolls-Royces. He walked over to the light blue Harley with the skulls, threw a leg across it and straddled the large leather seat. His dark eyes met mine as he nodded his head to the seat behind him. "Get on." I stepped forward and joined him, my hands instinctively wrapping around his waist.

"Where do you wanna go? To the stars? To the moon?"

I rested my head against his solid back. "How about into the sunset? I'll go anywhere as long as it's with you." I felt his chest rise and fall sharply as a heavy sigh escaped it.

"Come on, we have more to see."

I loosened my grip, and he helped me off the bike. Rejoining our hands, we continued on our journey. He guided me to the room where all his clothes were stored. He had personal seamstresses who kept his exact measurements and made his outlandish wardrobe.

"Do you prefer casual clothes or your onstage outfits?"

His reply was short and sweet. "I prefer being naked."

Such an ass. After leaving the clothing room, he guided me to his recording studio. We walked in and he flipped on the lights.

"And this is where the magic happens!"

I was in amazement and awe at all the soundboards and gadgets. There were microphones scattered throughout, along with drums, guitars, a piano and even a saxophone. They were all impressive. Sheets of music and scrawled notes were lying around everywhere. One of the walls was strictly dedicated to all of his platinum albums, and his vast collection of Grammy awards was sitting on a marble table next to it. I was thoroughly impressed with all of his accomplishments. He may have been an ass, but he was a talented ass. "Is this room soundproof?" I asked as I skimmed my finger across one of the golden Victrolas. My dirty mind was going off on a tangent.

He nodded slightly and flashed a slight smirk. "Yep."

As I went to question him more about the studio, he grabbed for my hand again. We quickly left and headed back towards the stairs leading up to the bedrooms.

"What exciting part of your world do I get to see next? That studio was cool!"

"The tour is over for today. It's time for you to get some sleep."

"But I'm not tired, Grayson."

He pulled me up the stairs, then turned down the hallway. Only we didn't stop at my bedroom door. We stopped at a room that was two more doors down. He wrapped his hand around the knob and opened it. I was in absolute shock as we walked inside. Every shade of blue imaginable decorated the room, with splashes of silver and gold mixed in. From the black four-poster king-size bed sitting on a cheetah print rug to the huge velvet draperies and over to the large bamboo palms surrounding the entirety. It was exquisite. It was definitely a room fit for rock royalty.

"Wow... what room is this?"

He slammed the door behind me. "Mine."

I walked over and sat down on the very end of the bed and watched as Grayson moved to a large sound system in the far corner of the room. He removed a record from the shelf and placed it on the turntable. After a couple of cracks and pops, the music came to life through the speakers. I immediately recognized the song as 'Unchained Melody' by The Righteous Brothers.

He turned around and walked back over to me, offering his hand. "Dance with me."

I accepted his hand, and he pulled me up, leading me to the middle of the room, our eyes never leaving each other. His arms snaked around my waist and he pressed his body tightly against mine. I enveloped him with my arms and glided my hands up his back, laying my head upon his chest. We swayed back and forth, lost in the song, lost in each other. I still wanted answers, but I didn't want to end the moment. He lowered his lips next to my ear and started singing.

Lonely rivers flow
To the sea, to the sea
To the open arms of the sea, yeah
Lonely rivers sigh
"Wait for me, wait for me"
I'll be coming home, wait for me

"Will you wait for me, Violet?"

The deep smoothness of his velvety voice mixed with the steady beat of his heart and his intoxicating scent lulled me off to dreamland. "Hmmm."

"Will you be patient with me?"

We stopped dancing, and I looked up at him through dreamy yet weary eyes,

"Yes Grayson, I will wait for you cause I —"

A loud yawn escaped me, and I felt my feet leave the floor.

"It's time for you to rest now."

A moment later, I was snuggling into the black and blue satin covers of Grayson's bed. The last thing I remember before closing my eyes was a pair of arms wrapping around me and a pair of lips softly kissing my neck.

CHAPTER TWENTY-SIX

The next morning, I awoke to the most wonderful smell. I tried to roll over and jump out of bed to follow the sweet aroma. But, I found that something big and furry blocked my legs and back. I deduced it must have been Grayson's pet, named Zeus. The large body pressed further against me as I moved my legs again. I extended a wary hand behind me and slowly petted the soft yet coarse pelt. A low chuff mixed with a deep grunting sound greeted my curious ears. This was definitely not a cat. So I assumed it was a dog. I continued stroking its fur as I made friendly conversation. "Hi Zeus, hi ya buddy. My name's Violet. I'm a friend of your daddy's. You sure are a big boy, huh? How about you let me turn around so I can get a good look at ya? Will you let me do that?"

I wiggled my legs until they were free enough so I could turn over in the bed. I scooted up a little against the pillow and turned to greet my new canine friend. "That's better. Ok buddy, how about we meet properly now?" I turned my head and came face to face with a... tiger! "AHHHHH! OH SHIT! You're not a dog... you're a... you're a..." I slowly climbed off the bed as a set of stunning yellow eyes stalked me. "Good kitty... you just stay right there," I pleaded, pushing my hands at humongous beast as I backed into the sold frame now standing behind me. I jumped.

"Morning baby, I see you've met Zeus!"

I turned around and looked up at him, my eyes full of terror and bewilderment. "Grayson! That's a tiger! You have a fucking tiger for a pet?! Jesus H. Christ!"

He threw his head back and roared with laughter. "Calm down Violet. He's a big baby. He won't hurt you."

My stomach growled in protest as I shook my head, threw my hands up, and headed downstairs. As I neared the kitchen, I discovered the source of the delicious smell. I walked into the dining room and found a huge plate of French toast with sausage and a glass of orange juice waiting for me on the table. I sat down and was getting ready to dig in when Grayson came up behind me, snaking his arms around my neck, kissing my cheek.

"Are you ok?"

I took a bite of sausage. "Really? What do you think?"

He sat down in the chair next to me.

"Ok, I'll give you that one. I guess it would be quite a shock to wake up next to a wild animal... well, with exception of me, that is." He laughed again.

I took a bite of French toast and a gulp of juice.

"How in the hell did you get a pet tiger?"

Grayson leaned back in his chair. "Well, when we were touring Asia, Zeus was part of a roadside attraction we came across. He was only a few months old then. There was just something special that drew me to him. I wanted to rescue him, but the dick owner wouldn't part with him."

I took another bite of food. "That's awful. I don't understand why or how people can be so cruel to animals. So, if the guy wouldn't give him to you, how did you end up with him?"

He grabbed my juice and took a drink. "I offered him money. Cold hard cash. And while he grabbed the money, I grabbed Zeus. Well, actually Rob grabbed him and arranged for him to stay at a wildlife rescue there in India until he could be flown here to New York. It cost me a lot of money to make it all legit, but he's worth every penny."

"Aww, it sounds like you love him a lot. And I'm sure he loves you too for saving him. You're a good man, Charlie Brown."

Grayson chuckled. "Yeah, I guess so. But it looks like he loves someone else now."

Just then I felt familiar fur brush against me. It was Zeus.

"Go ahead Violet... pet him."

I laid down my fork and nervously reached to caress his massive head. He pushed it into my head and purred. Loudly. It was a very surreal moment. Never in my wildest dreams would I have ever imagined being in the same room as a tiger, let alone petting one. He was so gentle and loving. "Are you my new friend, Zeus?" His pink tongue encircled my hand while I stroked him. I won't lie, though. I was still a little wary that he might have eaten my hand.

Grayson was beaming. "See, I told you there's nothing to be afraid of."

After one final head-but and chuff, Zeus was on his way toward the French patio doors that lead to the backyard. Grayson got up to let him out and quickly returned.

"I still can't believe what I just experienced." I shook my head again. "And I can't believe that you made me breakfast."

Grayson laughed. "The perks of being rich and famous baby. And, sorry to burst your bubble, but I didn't make your food. Chef did. The only things I can cook are omelets."

"Well, that's something, isn't it?"

He shook his head. "Not if you ask the people who ate them."

I giggled at him. "Well, thank you anyway."

He got up and disappeared into the kitchen, returning with a mug of coffee nestled in his hand. He sat back down and stared at me. "You're welcome. Did you sleep well?"

I washed down the rest of my juice. "Yes. But I don't remember much about last night. I remember touring the house, then going to your room, and then it's kind of hazy from there."

Grayson took a sip, then cleared his throat. "Do you remember us dancing together?" He paused. "Or talking?"

I shook my head no. "I remember we danced and then I was lying in your bed, sorry."

"It's alright. Look, I will be in rehearsal and the studio for most of the day. But we are going out on the town tonight. So," he reached into the leather wallet lying in front of him on the table, "I want you to go shopping and pick out something beautiful." He handed me his American Express Onyx card. "Get whatever you need. Price is no object. If you have any problems, call Rob. Charles will wait to drive you when you are ready."

I shoved it back at him. "Grayson I can't take —"

"Yes, you can. Now be a good girl and do as I say."

I conceded and accepted the card. "Yes, sir."

That familiar devilish smirk appeared on his lips. "That's right." He leaned over and crashed his lips against mine. "I'll see you later."

I finished my breakfast, then returned to my room to get dressed. When I was ready, I stepped out into the crisp Manhattan air and Charles greeted me.

"Morning' Miss Violet. Where are you off to?"

"Well, Charles, I need to buy a nice dress for tonight. Do you know of any places?"

He opened the back door on the sedan. "Sure do. Hop in."

I climbed into the black Cadillac and soon we were off. About an hour later, we pulled up to a small boutique. Charles helped me out of the car and I told him I would try not to take too long. I entered the boutique and the friendly saleslady who greeted me offered to help find the perfect dress. The one I settled on was elegant and sophisticated. I fell in love with it, and I hoped Grayson did, too. Once I found matching shoes, a clutch, and some jewelry, the poor black plastic card had suffered almost two thousand dollars worth of damage. I felt bad about spending so much, but he told me to get something nice. Maybe he would let me pay him back. I exited the store and returned to the car, headed back to the Manor.

***

I climbed the balcony staircase back to my bedroom and dropped my shopping bags and boxes on the bed. Opening the ivory boutique box, I pulled out the dress and walked to the closet. Grabbing a hanger, I tucked it inside the dress and draped the cape across the top. I returned to the bed and pulled out the velvet box that held my necklace, earrings, and bracelet and laid it on the dresser. As I went back to open the bag containing my heels, I heard the ringing of a telephone. I waited to see if someone would answer it, but it continued to ring excessively. I followed the ringing out into the hallway and made a right, walking all the way down. There was a door that was propped halfway open, so I pushed it and stepped inside. It appeared to be an office. I moved to stand next to the desk that was there and hesitated momentarily before picking up the red receiver.

"Hello?" I answered lowly.

"Who the fuck is this?" A woman's voice screamed on the other end.

"Violet. Who's this?"

"Well, Violet, this is none of your damn business. Where is Grayson, and why are you answering his phone?"

I just stood there, dumbfounded. Was this the bitch that he was talking to yesterday? I opened my mouth to say something, but the sound of another voice scared the shit out of me.

"Violet! What are you doing in here?"

It was Rob.

"Hang up that phone and come out of there."

I dropped the receiver on its cradle and scurried out.

"Girl, you were about to give me a heart attack! That's the boss's personal office. Nobody is allowed in there unless he invites them."

"Sorry, I heard the phone ringing and nobody answered it, so I did."

Rob shook his head. "Yeah, and that's another thing. Never ever answer the phones in this house. The boss has them everywhere. But only he is can use them. Who was it anyway?"

I darted my gaze from Rob to the floor. "Some woman looking for Grayson."

Rob sighed and nodded slightly. "That's nothing new. They call and show up here all the time." He patted my shoulder. "I'm sorry, Violet, as much as you don't need or want to hear that, it's the truth."

I gave him a half-hearted smile. "It's ok Rob. I know it's just rock 'n' roll. It's the lifestyle that Grayson is used to, and I'm not here to change it."

The pain in my heart was grabbing hold again. I turned away from him and headed back to my room. I laid down across the bed and let the tears flow until I fell asleep.

***

Sometime later, a knock on the door roused me, and I sleepily called out.

"Who is it?"

"Violet it's Rob. I came to check on you and let you know that the boss wants you to arrive at the restaurant at eight o'clock."

"Ok," I yawned. "What time is it now?"

"It's six thirty. I'll let Charles know. Just come down when you're ready."

"Alright. Thank you."

Rolling out of bed, I headed for the bathroom. After showering, I retrieved my dress, cape, and matching heels. I slid on the dress and heels, then walked over to the dresser, opening the black velvet box on top of it. Taking the clasp of the rose-colored pendant, I secured it around my neck. I then pinned the small diamond earrings to my earlobes and decorated my wrist with the sapphire cuff. After adding a few small curls to my hair, I placed it into an elegant bun on the top of my head. I painted my eyes and lips, then grabbed the cape before heading downstairs. Arriving at the main door, Charles greeted me.

"You look absolutely stunning, Miss Violet! Mr. Maddox will be thrilled."

I blushed. "Thank you, Charles."

He helped me into the car, and we were on our way.

CHAPTER TWENTY-SEVEN

Almost an hour later, we arrived at a fancy restaurant called La Belle. Charles helped me out of the car and escorted me to the door. I entered the establishment and met the Maître D'.

"Good evening, Madam. Welcome to La Belle. May I have your name, please?"

I stepped forward. "Hello, yes, I'm here to meet Mr. Maddox."

The older balding man in the tuxedo scrutinized the book in front of him. "Ah yes, Mr. Maddox has a reservation this evening. He has asked for a private table. Right this way."

I followed behind him as he led me to a secluded table next to the main dining area. He pulled out my chair, and I sat down.

"Would you like to order something or wait for your companion?"

"Just a glass of Merlot will be fine. Thank you."

"Of course."

Not long after, a waiter appeared with my wine. I slowly sipped as I continuously scanned the room, waiting for Grayson to arrive. I hoped he would come soon.

When the waiter returned with my third glass, I knew something wasn't right. "Excuse me, can you tell me what time it is?"

He sat the glass down and glanced at his watch. "Yes ma'am, it is nine twenty."

I sighed. "Thank you."

"Would you like me to place an order for you now?"

"Not yet. I am still waiting for —"

"Yes, I will order for both of us. Please bring two plates of the Lasagne Florentine."

"Very good, sir."

The waiter headed toward the kitchen, and Grayson sat down across from me.

"Where have you been? You said you would be here at eight?"

He took a sip of his water. "Why? You writin' a book?"

He was pissing me off already. And this shitty attitude of his had to go.

"No, but when you tell someone to meet you at a specific time, you don't show up an hour and a half late without a reasonable explanation. Or is that how they do it in Hollywood?"

He bore his aggravated eyes into mine. "I was busy. There's your explanation."

"That's not an excuse, Grayson."

"Is for me. I'm a star, baby. It goes with the territory."

I released a half sigh, half growl as the waiter returned with our entrees, presented them to us and nodded. "Please enjoy!"

Grayson and I ate in silence. Each time I opened my mouth to say something to him, I stopped. I would rather spend my time with him eating in silence then to spend it arguing. Midway through our dinner, I excused myself to use the ladies' room. He didn't seem to care, and I needed a break from his childishness. I entered the bathroom and immediately noticed a familiar face.

"Buffy?"

She finished touching up her lipstick, then turned toward me.

"Hi Violet!"

We embraced in a light hug.

"It's been a while. What are you doing here?"

"Biff had a business meeting today, and he brought me here for dinner before we fly back to Chicago. He's been a real doll lately, dropping money on me left and right. I feel like a princess."

I scoffed and rolled my eyes. "Hmmm."

Buffy's face filled with concerned. "Are you ok?"

I really didn't want to say anything, but I needed to vent. "Not really. You know Buffy, I have come to the conclusion that all men are nothing but dogs!"

She patted me on the shoulder. "I'm sorry to hear that, sweetie. You're a nice girl. I hope whoever this dog is, you're referring to, realizes that. And if not, forget about him. I'm so lucky to have my Biff. I don't know what I would do without him." She smiled brightly.

I didn't want to burst her bubble and hurt her. But I allowed my pain to control my thinking and the filter guarding my mouth vanished.

"Biff isn't as wonderful as you think, Buffy."

Her face twisted in anger, and she laid into me. "What the hell do you mean by that? You really have no room to talk. He has given you numerous chances and has allowed you to keep your job when you should have been fired a long time ago!"

I took a step back from her. As much as I wanted to get into the whole work subject, I didn't. But she needed to know that Biff wasn't the man she thought he was.

"I'm not talking about work. Look, I really didn't want to say anything, but you need to know. Last week I was at the mall and I saw Biff with another woman. It was Dottie Meyers. They had lunch together, then walked through the mall holding hands." I didn't dare tell her how I followed them and about the scene in Sears. The shock and hurt on her face were enough.

"You don't know what you're talking about! Biff would never hurt me! And especially with her!"

My mouth continued to run. "I'm sorry Buffy, it's true. He even bought her a huge bouquet of flowers and they spend a lot of time together in his office. The last thing I want to do is hurt you, but us women have to stick together. You needed to know."

Buffy opened her purse and threw the tube of pink lipstick into it, continuing to throw daggers at me as she walked toward the exit.

"You know what Violet, you're just jealous. That's all it is. You can't find a decent man, so you're trying to make anyone that is happy feel miserable. Well, screw you!"

The bathroom door violently swung open, then slammed shut.

I sighed and turned to face myself in the mirror. Was I wrong to tell her? Maybe I was and maybe I wasn't. I took a deep breath and started on my way back to dinner with Mr. Personality. I exited the bathroom and an enormous hand clasped around my throat, shoving me back into a corner.

"You bitch! Why did you tell Buffy I was with Dottie?"

I looked up into the terrifying steel-blue eyes of Biff. My body was shaking like a leaf and my breathing was erratic. My mind flashed back to the moment I was raped. "Because you were, and she needed to know that the sun doesn't rise and set on you!" I spat at him in a raspy voice.

His oversized fingers pressed deeper against my trachea. "I told you to mind your own fucking business if you knew what was good for you! You don't listen, do you?"

My chest was burning as I forced shallow breaths in and out of it, my eyes rolling to the back of my head.

"Answer me, you whore!"

My voice was barely audible. "No."

Just as my world was about to turn black, Biff loosened his death grip.

"You better keep your fucking mouth shut about this! Do you understand?"

I nodded as I took a huge breath and reached for my neck, rubbing the now swelling flesh there.

"Good!"

He turned and walked away from me, returning to his table.

I was on the verge of tears as I rejoined Grayson. I sat down and he looked at me.

"Damn, I thought you fell in," he chuckled, finishing his dinner.

I said nothing as my throat was killing me. I reached for my water glass and tried to take a sip, but I couldn't and started choking.

"Are you ok baby? Look, I'm sorry about earlier. I'm just a little on edge with the whole tour thing."

I couldn't hold back the tears anymore as he met my emotional eyes.

"Why are you crying? I said I was sorry."

"I ran into Buffy Cartwell in the bathroom." My words were hoarse and squeaky.

"What's wrong with your voice?"

"I told her that Biff was having an affair. She must have told him cause when I came out of the bathroom..." I cried even harder and returned my hand to my neck.

"What happened Violet?" The concern flavoring Grayson's tone slowly turned to dark anger.

I swallowed hard, and through my tears, I told him. "He grabbed me by my throat and shoved me into a corner. He threatened me."

Grayson quietly pushed his chair back from the table and stood up, throwing his cloth napkin on his plate. He motioned for a waiter, whispered something in his ear, then walked away with him. I jumped up and followed behind them. We returned to the main dining area, coming to a stop at the table by the fireplace.

"Well, hi there Violet! What are you doing here? It sure is a small world." Biff's eyes darted to Grayson, and he laughed. Buffy just sat there.

Grayson's body started quaking as he unleashed his fury on Biff.

"So, you like to hide out in women's bathrooms and attack them when they come out? You fuckin' coward! You need to stay the hell away from her or else!"

Biff laughed again as he pushed back from the table and stood in front of Grayson. "Aww Violet, that's so sweet. Your over-the-hill gee-tar picker is standing up for you." He pushed his large hand against Grayson's chest, rocking him backwards. "Or else what? You ain't gonna do shit, you flamboyant pussy!"

The sudden sound of knuckles meeting jawbone shattered the relaxing, jazz filled atmosphere of La Belle. "That's for Violet!"

Buffy flew out of her chair as Biff started rocking.

"Oh my God! Biff baby!" She looked at Grayson. "You animal!"

The sudden commotion caused the other patrons to gather around and I heard the Maître D' yell for someone to call the police. My tears rained harder as I begged Grayson to stop.

"Baby, please, no more! The police are on their way. I don't want you to go to jail!"

He spun around and cast an evil look at me. "Just back off! He's mine!"

Before Biff could get his bearings, my dark lover reared back again and hit him with a shot right between the eyes. This time he fell to the floor, the blood from his now shattered nose joining the blood from his busted jaw. Grayson finished him with a hard kick between the legs, in the balls. David had defeated Goliath.

"And that's for calling me flamboyant!"

While Biff lay on his side whimpering in pain, Grayson continued. "Don't you ever come near her again, motherfucker. Cause if you do… I'll kill you myself! That's a promise! And you need to find a new assistant cause she quits!"

The entire scene left me an emotional mess. I took off and ran out of the restaurant to the car. I jerked the back door open and jumped in, not waiting for Charles. I was still crying and shaking. I couldn't believe what just transpired. A minute later, the door opened and Grayson climbed in. The door barely clicked shut as we sped off into the night.

"You're welcome!" he huffed, reaching into the wine bucket for a chunk of ice, rubbing it across both hands.

I didn't know how to feel.

"I can't believe you just did that. You're gonna be in trouble now, and I don't think I can deal with that."

"He ain't gonna do anything," Grayson scoffed, shaking his head. "And really Violet? That's the thanks I get for defending your honor? That's straight up bullshit!"

I turned in my seat to stare out the tinted window. The awkward quietness between us was almost deafening. It wasn't too long before we were pulling back up to the front door of the Manor. Charles parked the car, and I jumped out, stalking inside, heading straight for the stairs. Grayson was hot on my trail. When I reached my room, I immediately started stripping off my clothes. I took off my jewelry and laid it on the dresser. As I reached inside the top drawer for my nightgown, he walked in and leaned his slender frame up against the door.

"I had dinner and now I see my desert."

I flashed him an angry look as I smoothed the gown across my body.

"What the fuck is wrong with you? You haven't said two words."

And what happens when someone dances one too many times on top of a landmine? Kaboom.

I turned around and unleashed my pent up frustration.

"What the fuck is wrong with *me*? I'll tell you. As much as I appreciate what you just did, you shouldn't have had to resort to violence. And how dare you just make life decisions for me? How could you tell him I quit? I should have done that myself! What am I going to do about work now? And furthermore, you still haven't answered my questions from yesterday! I can't just assume your feelings, if there are any, for me. I'm not a fucking mind reader, Grayson."

"You can always find another job, Violet. Hell, you can work for me. Why are you always sticking up for that bastard Biff? This isn't the first time you've done it. Are you fucking him too?"

My blood boiled in my veins, and hot tears were scorching my eyes. How dare he say that!

"Really Grayson? Ok, if you want to go there then we will. I should be asking you that question. Who have *you* been fucking?"

He looked taken aback. "What are you talking about? I haven't been with anyone. I've been rehearsing and you know that. Where's this comin' from?"

"Nevermind," I huffed as I walked over to the bed and sat down. He followed and stood in front of me.

"I asked you a question." His tone was low and demanding.

"Fine, if you wanna know, I heard you having a conversation with some woman yesterday at the front door. I heard the things she was saying, Grayson, about you and her. Then, I answered the phone today and there was a woman on the other end asking for you. She wanted to know who I was and got upset. It was probably the same girl."

"You answered my phone? Baby, you need to learn that some things just shouldn't concern you."

I jumped up from the bed and stormed toward the closet. "Oh really? I shouldn't be concerned? How do I know you aren't sleeping around? I know that your fame brings you anything, and anyone, that you want, but I will not stand by and wait in line with the rest of them. It's all or nothing with me!"

I jerked up my suitcases and threw them on the bed, unzipping them.

"What are you doing?"

I bore a hole through him as I walked over to the closet and slid the door open, ripping my clothes off the hangers, slamming them in the large suitcase. "What the hell does it look like? I'm packing. I think it's time I go back to Chicago."

I continued to devoid the closet of my clothes and shoes, then walked over to the dresser and emptied it too. As I walked into the bathroom to retrieve my personal items, I almost broke down. I couldn't believe that he was just going to stand there and watch me pack, watch me walk out of his life... forever. I honestly wanted his heart to ache, just like mine did when he walked out on me.

I returned to the bedroom and deposited my items into the smaller suitcase, zipping it shut. I knew he was still staring at me, but I couldn't look at him. If I did, that would be it. I needed to be strong. I placed the last piece of clothing I had in the large suitcase and zipped it up. Just as I was about to pick it up and set it on the floor, another hand grabbed the handle and I watched as my suitcase went flying across the room, smashing into the glass door of the closet.

I jumped and started shaking. "Grayson! Oh my God! What are you doing?!"

He reached for the second bag and sent it flying across the room to join the first one. His calloused fingers dug into my shoulders, holding them in a vice-like grip as he turned me to face him. His hazel orbs were burning with anger and... lust. Suddenly, in one swift motion, he wrapped his hands around my waist and hoisted me up, flinging me across his shoulder. He stalked toward the door and we entered the hallway. Heading to the staircase, we quickly descended them. Once we reached the first floor, Grayson carried me down another hallway to a door at the very end.

"There's one room I forgot to show you on our tour, Violet," his words crossed his lips in a dark and dangerous tone, "but I think you'll like it."

He unlocked the door, opened it, and we descended another flight of stairs. The room was dark at first, but I could faintly see light the closer we got to the bottom. Grayson placed his hand against my back as he bent down and sat me on my feet. I raised my head and looked around. The sight that my eyes absorbed and my brain tried to comprehend left me in utter shock. Grayson swept up behind me and placed his lips against my ear, whispering deeply.

"Welcome to *my* dungeon..."

CHAPTER TWENTY-EIGHT

My eyes slowly scanned my surroundings. From the collection of torturous devices hanging on the wall, to the oversized furniture and sex swing, over to the wire cage, and finally to the gorgeous bed, it was all absolutely amazing. The red and black décor was very erotic, yet classy. I couldn't believe that Grayson had this hidden away in his basement. When he came to me that night and said he was curious about my world, I had no inkling of the secret that he himself had been keeping.

"You love it, don't you?" he whispered again. "I've only brought a handful of people down here. None of them could last. They said I was crazy. But not you, Violet. You're the only one who understands."

At that point, I didn't care what he said. I loved the room, but I was in no mood to play. I walked over to the side of the bed and sat down. My face instantly fell into my hands and I cried uncontrollably. My throat still hurt from Biff's surprise attack, and my mind and heart were weary and broken.

"Please stop crying, Violet." His voice was a quiet demand.

I raised my head. "I can't."

I felt the bed dip as Grayson sat down next to me.

"Please look at me." He almost sounded like he was pleading.

I continued crying and stared straight ahead.

His soft hands reached for my face, turning it to meet his. "I'm sorry Violet. I'm so damn sorry."

My tears rained down harder onto my cheeks, flowing like a river across his fingers, as I shook my head.

"You just don't understand."

His hazel orbs burned into my emerald ones. "I understand a lot more than you think. I know how you feel about me. And last night when we were dancing, you almost told me you —"

I sniffled. "That I what Grayson?"

He let go of my face and lowered his head, shaking it. "It doesn't matter now."

I got up from the bed and stood before him. Reaching for his head, I cradled it between my hands, my eyes burning his image to my retinas, my memory. The small pieces of my heart that remained unbroken finally shattered at the next words I uttered.

"I'm sorry that I'm not what you want." The words left my lips in an almost hushed tone. "I hope that one day, you will allow yourself to open up and be loved by someone completely. I hope you find a love that makes you want to fight for it, no matter the cost."

My devastated sobs echoed off the soundproof padding as my body shook.

"And when you find that love, please hold on to it with every fiber of your being. Make the woman you truly love, your one and only. Treasure her and cherish her. Never let her go, because she is your true soulmate… Eugene."

Looking at him one last time, I released my hold and headed back toward the staircase. The room was silent before an ear-piercing scream shattered it.

"NO!"

I jumped slightly at the crashing noises behind me, but kept going. I could tell by the sound that Grayson was destroying something. He screamed again.

"FUCK!"

My foot was about to touch the final step when he called out.

"Violet wait!"

I stopped.

"Please… don't go. I need you."

I processed his words, trying to decide if he was being honest. I turned around and listened to what he had to say.

"I care for you, too. My feelings are so damn deep that they scare me. You want me for the person that I am, not the superstar. I've only felt this way about one other woman and when it ended, I never wanted to feel that pain again. But then you came into my life and awakened my heart. I'm sorry that I walked out on you. I'm sorry that I hurt you."

He ran a hand through his soft brown hair, lowering his eyes for a moment before returning my gaze.

"You have to understand that I'm not good at the whole relationship thing. My parents weren't a very good example for me. I'm not sure if I can give you what you want or deserve. I've been fucked up in the head since I was a kid. I've got so much pain and darkness locked away inside. My music is my main source of release, but sometimes I want so much more. I know I don't always make the best decisions, no matter how right I think I am. And I know that sex is a big part of my life, and I have been with a lot of girls, but there is only one woman who has seen through my bullshit and reaches me deep down inside. There is only one woman who I would give it all up for."

I watched his chest rise and fall as a choked sob crossed his lips. "I don't want to lose you, Violet. You're a part of me now."

My own tears were flowing again as I ran back down the stairs and embraced him tightly. I had waited for so long to hear those words and I knew it took a lot for him to speak them. I looked up into his beautiful eyes and saw nothing but sincerity. I placed my hands against his face and collected the tears streaming down his cheeks, sweeping them away with my thumbs. We both sniffled as he lowered his head to capture my lips in a tender but sensual kiss. When we pulled away, he smiled that gorgeous smile of his. "I meant every word I said."

The joy filling my heart radiated to my face. "I know baby, I know."

I reached for his hand and guided him to the bed, sitting down. It was a big step for him to open up to me. I just hoped that he would continue to let me in.

"You don't have to answer me if you're not ready, but what happened to you as a kid?"

Grayson looked away, then turned back to me.

"You can tell me anything, baby. I'm right here."

He swallowed hard and a perplexed look crossed his face, as if he didn't know where to start.

"I really don't want to go into detail but I'll say that a lot of my issues come from watching my parents fight, being verbally and physically abused, problems with my stepfather, my father kicking me out of his house, and all the ridicule and teasing I've endured."

I shook my head. "I've never understood how some parents can treat their own flesh and blood the way they do." Reaching for his hand, I enveloped it in my own. "I'm sorry you had to go through so much. But you know what? You're a survivor, just like me. Everything you have experienced has made you a stronger person and brought you to this point in your life. Your music not only helps people have a good time, it also helps them through their own pain."

He shrugged his shoulders. "I guess. Maybe one day I'll be ready to tell you everything." He smiled half-heartedly at me. "Maybe one day I can learn to let go of the pain."

The emotion in his eyes and words tore at me. I couldn't change anything that he had been through or take his pain away completely, but I could help him relieve some of it. Making my decision, I stood up and gingerly reached for the straps of my nightgown, smoothed them over my arms, and let the sheer fabric fall to the floor.

"What are you do —"

I placed a fire-engine red fingernail to Grayson's lips. "Shhh."

Walking over to the table next to the other side of the bed, I picked up the familiar collar laying there and buckled it around my neck. I walked back over and stood before him. His eyes were still emotional, but they were filling with sparks of curiosity and desire.

"Use me."

My words were simple but held so much power.

"What do you mean?"

"You have so much inside of you that needs to be released. I can help with that."

"I can't let you do that, Violet." His voice lowered. "My issues are too dark."

"If we're going to start a relationship, it has to be built on trust."

His fingers reached for the swollen bruise on my neck and smoothed across it. "What if I hurt you?"

I placed my hand on top of his, looking at him sincerely. "I trust you."

Uneasiness and hesitancy filled his eyes. I knew he wouldn't be able to take the initiative himself, so I would have to start the ball rolling. Violet disappeared as Mistress Crimson once again took over. Only this time, I was just leading him.

"What the fuck are you waiting for?" My hand slammed against him, pushing into his chest.

A flash went off in his dark eyes.

"Maybe Biff was right..."

His face twisted in anger, and he shook.

"You are a pussy!"

That was all it took.

Grayson snapped and dug his fingers into the soft flesh of my arm, dragging me across the room to the black leather table. Throwing me face down, he secured my wrists and ankles with four metal chains. I started wiggling against the restraints and he pulled them tighter.

"OW!"

His firm hand unleashed a stinging blow against my bare ass.

"Shut up Marie! You bitch! You're my mother. How could you love him more than me?"

I spat at him. "Fuck you Eugene!"

I heard him walk away and knew he had returned when I felt the swift smack of leather balls against my back.

SWOOSH

I recognized the instrument as a cat-o'-nine-tails.

"Is that all you got? No wonder your parents didn't want you. You hit like a damn girl!"

His hand came down harder.

SWOOSH

"I'm a good kid! Why can't they see that? Why doesn't anyone want me?"

"You ain't good at shit! Nobody wants your sorry ass!"

He stopped and disappeared again. I was getting a little nervous until I felt the crashing pain of a metal rod as it met my spine.

CRACK

"They all need to shut up!"

CRACK

"I just wanna be like everyone else!" He started crying

CRACK

I unleashed a wicked laugh.

"Oh, boo hoo. You cry like a fucking girl!"

He brought down one last blow before unlocking the shackles. He ripped his fingers through my long locks and jerked me up from the table. Dragging me across the room, he threw me down on the large black sex cushion and bent me over it, spreading my legs.

"What are you gonna do now, *Barbie*?"

A demonic laugh left his chest. "You're about to find out!"

He was gone for only a few seconds before I felt the softness of his trousers press against my cheeks. In one swift motion, he pried them open and rammed something hard deep inside my ass.

"OW FUCK!" The pain was excruciating. He didn't use any lube.

"What's the matter Jim? Can't handle it? You don't lock little boys in rooms and leave them!"

I gnashed my teeth together and breathed through the pain. "Oh, I can handle it. And your obsession with assholes makes me think you may not like just girls!"

Grayson pushed the dildo deeper inside of me, twisting it.

"Don't say that!" he growled.

The pain increased in intensity and my tears flowed as he now began fucking my ass with the hard object, tearing me wide. All the way out, then all the way back in, over and over. Just when I didn't think my body could take anymore, he pulled it out and jerked me up by my hair again. This time he dragged me over to the Saint Andrew's cross next to the cage and threw me against it, strapping my feet to the bottom and my wrists to the top, leaving me spread eagle. I watched as he sauntered back over to the device rack, picked up his next tool, and stalked back toward me.

"And this right here," he smoothed the end of the whip through his fingers, "is for you, Father!"

I stared him dead in the eye. "You ain't gonna do shit boy, cause you ain't shit!"

My dark lover brought his face mere inches from mine. "TRY ME!"

I spit in his face.

He reared back and backhanded me across the face. The pain shooting through my body made my head fall to the side. I slowly gained my bearings and turned to face him.

Whaahh-psssh

The crack of the whip echoed throughout the room as it seared my bare breasts. I closed my eyes and whimpered.

Whaahh-psssh

He cracked it again, this time across my upper thighs and legs.

He reared back one last time with all his might and unleashed a lashing across my stomach and pussy.

Whaahh-psssh

I screamed out as the pain rocked me. I hung my head and let the tears flow. The welts on my body were bleeding and the bruises on my back and neck were burning. I didn't know how much more I could physically take. But if it was helping Grayson, then I would have kept at it forever. But right now, I couldn't move. And I had to tell him about the concern I had for him hitting my stomach. But given the state of mind he was in, would he care? I suddenly felt a set of hands sweep my hair back from my face and caress it. My weary eyes locked with the emotional and concerned eyes of my lover.

"Oh my God... Violet baby, what have I done?"

I was on the verge of passing out. But before I did, I had to tell him. I felt my arms and feet go loose as he freed them. Wrapping his hands around my waist, he picked me up and carried me in his arms over to the bed, gently laying me down on the soft duvet. My body went limp and my eyes fluttered shut. He stroked my hair one more time, and I felt his lips lightly pecking mine.

"Violet, can you hear me? Answer me! I told you I would hurt you. Why did you let me do this?"

With all the strength I could muster, I opened my eyes one last time and looked at him. The words flowing across my lips wafted through the air and against his ears in a hushed tone.

"I'm pregnant..."

The world then went black.

Scarlet Robbins is the author of The Senses Series (paranormal romance), The Rock Chronicles (erotica), and The Collection of Thoughts poetry collection. Originally from the East Coast, she now resides in the Midwest. She describes the perfect day of writing as listening to the sound of falling rain, while sipping tea, with her yellow Labrador, Barney-Bear (a.k.a. Doof) by her side.

To keep up with Scarlet be sure to visit:
www.scarletrobbins.com
Twitter: @scarletauthor
Instagram: scarletrobbinsauthor

CPSIA information can be obtained
at www.ICGtesting.com
Printed in the USA
BVHW032124230922
647846BV00012B/547